Storm

Lou Cadle

Storm
Copyright © 2016 by Cadle-Sparks Books

http://www.loucadle.com

Books by Lou Cadle

The Gray Series:
Gray, Part I
Gray, Part II
Gray, Part III

Erupt
Quake
Storm

41 Days: Apocalypse Underground

Crow Vector (May 2017)

The Dawn of Mammals Series:
Saber Tooth
Terror Crane
Hell Pig
Killer Pack
Mammoth

Audio books:

The Gray Series (coming soon)

*Dedicated to the first responders—police, fire, medical, and more—
who put our needs ahead of their own families' in disasters.
Thank you.*

Captain T

It's early in this April morning and the sky is beautiful, blue, with a few fair-weather cumulus, but deceptively nice weather, I promise. You can feel the humidity in the air already here in Terre Haute, Indiana, where the college girls are smokin' and loving being outdoors in shorts again. I'm loving that too, needless to say.

Captain T—that's T for tornado—doesn't enjoy getting up this early, but after last evening's multiple tornados in Missouri and across into Illinois, he knew he had to chase this weather front through its second day. Radar loops showed less activity in the cooler hours, which long-time tornado fans know is common, but the line is still active, and the day's warming will spin up more twisters. Humid air flows up from the Gulf—it's blowing through the Cap's blond locks right now as you can see—and the upper levels are bringing us that cold Canadian air. A recipe for awesomeness.

Can't promise you EF3s and above, but it looks like we'll get more daylight action today than yesterday. Videographer sidekick says yeah to that, don't you, Felix? (Camera moves as if nodding.)

It's Captain T, extreme chaser, signing off for now. Catch you later on the dryline.

(Posted at YouTube and CaptainTforTornado.com)

Chapter 1

Greg Duncan barely noticed the weather as he trudged up the walk to his house. He unlocked both locks and opened the door to the distant sound of *Little Bear* coming out of the TV. He followed the noise into the living room and stood for a moment, watching his daughter, Holly, as she sat with one white sock on and one dangling from her hand, mesmerized at the cartoon.

"Heya, kiddo," he said, walking over to plant a kiss on the back of her neck over the collar of her school uniform shirt.

"You're scratchy, Dad," said Holly.

"And sweaty and gross," he said, standing up.

"Mmm," she said, her attention back on the cartoon.

"Finish getting dressed," Greg said, feeling that wild rush of love for her that half-scared him with its power. It came at the strangest times—not just when she was being good or sweet or funny, but at random moments when she didn't even know she had his attention. He watched her for a few more seconds, indulging himself, then left the room.

In the kitchen, he found Malika doing dishes. "Hi, Mr. Duncan," she said. "I turned your coffee on when I heard you drive up."

"Thanks. How'd the night go?"

"Great. Peaceful."

"Good. Get your homework done?"

"Always," she said. "And before you ask, no, Holly's mom didn't call."

He nodded. It figured.

"Want eggs?" Malika asked. "Cereal?"

"No, thanks. I've got a breakfast date."

"Really?" She turned, wiping her hands on a dish towel. "A date?"

He shook his head. "Not that sort. With my aunt."

"Oh."

"Like I have time for the other."

"I know what you mean." Malika's face was serious—as it often was. It was easy to forget she wasn't yet eighteen. She looked and acted much older. "I'll go get Holly."

He felt a familiar guilty twinge about being on the night shift. Couldn't be helped, but he'd rather not leave the teenager in charge all night. With any babysitter other than Malika, he wouldn't, though in his prowl car he could rush back home in a minute or two from anywhere in town. The situation, he knew, was less than ideal. But it'd be worse for him and Holly in the autumn, when Malika would be off at college.

Greg really didn't want to think about that. Finding a new babysitter half as good as Malika would be nearly impossible. He'd no doubt need to find an adult, and he'd be paying twice as much too, money he really didn't have.

Later. Think about today's problems today and save those worries for the summer, when the search for a new babysitter would have to begin.

He heard the television go off, and Malika steered Holly into the kitchen.

Greg took the milk carton out of the fridge and put it on the table. He pointed to the cartoon cow on it. "Hey, Holly, what do cows watch on TV?"

"Moooovies." She giggled.

Malika shook her head. "Groan," she said, smiling as she poured out cereal for Holly.

Greg watched Holly eat while he sipped his coffee. She was going through a dawdling phase. It wasn't about disliking school, he was pretty sure. She just took her sweet time about everything, and there was no hurrying her.

At the rate she was eating her cereal, they'd be late for school. He put a banana on the table to remind himself to take it along. Maybe she'd eat a few bites on the ride.

While Malika convinced Holly to finish putting on her shoes, Greg changed his uniform for a plaid flannel shirt and jeans. He helped Holly with her backpack, grabbed the banana, and hustled them all out the door, no more than five minutes late. After dropping Malika at Fidelity Community High, he drove Holly to the grade school, where she joined the other stragglers walking up the steps. A honk behind him forced him to continue on around the semi-circle drive before he could watch her walk all the way inside.

He made a last stop at Malika's mom's apartment.

He rang the doorbell, waited a minute, and rang it again. Finally, Darla Jefferson opened the door, pulling a worn blue plush robe tighter around her chunky middle.

"Ms. Jefferson," he said. "Here's Malika's things." He set the duffle bag inside the door.

"Would you like to come in?" she said.

"I'm sorry, no. I have to get going."

She gave a curt nod. "I heard from Antoine last night."

Her only son, in a work release program in Columbus. "How's he doing?"

"He says it's hard work."

Greg wasn't sure what he was supposed to say to that. Was it a complaint?

"I wish he could be here," she said.

Here was where he got in trouble, so he was probably better off somewhere else. Greg didn't say it, though it was true. Instead, he said. "I'm sure you miss him. But Columbus isn't far. Maybe you can visit soon."

"If I didn't have the others," she said—meaning Malika and her sister, twelve years old and not nearly as bright as Malika, from the hints Malika had given. "It's so much work."

Greg felt himself getting impatient with her weary tone. "I gotta go. Have a nice day, now."

As he trotted back to his car, he felt guilty about his impatience. He should have more sympathy for her.

He *did* have sympathy for her—in theory. It was harder to have sympathy after a few minutes in her actual presence. She had three children by two men, neither of which had stayed for long. She had been born into poverty and lived in poverty still. A recipe for disaster, which Antoine, Malika's half-brother, had acted out as if following a script, getting into enough trouble that he had ended up in juvie. Greg hadn't arrested him—thank God—but the kid had committed a robbery. Malika said—and Greg was willing to believe—he had intended a burglary only, with no threat of violence, but the boy he was with hadn't had the same plan. Both were prosecuted for robbery and plea bargained. The older boy had gone to prison and Antoine to juvie.

The best he had been able to do for Malika was help get her brother into a work-release program, a trade apprenticeship deal in Columbus. The kid—young man, now—was learning masonry.

Greg hoped he'd straighten himself out. He hoped Malika wouldn't end up bailing him out of jail the whole rest of her life, or feeling compelled to visit him in prison. Malika was the hope of the family, smart and hardworking and never in trouble. Her mother had given up long ago.

She might deserve to feel self-pity, but Greg wished the woman would find some gumption in herself, learn a lesson from her hardworking daughter, and take responsibility for making herself a better future.

He sighed. He had done what he could for that family, and he needed to let it go. It wasn't his problem, right?

If not, why did he always feel that it somehow was? That he hadn't done enough?

* * *

His mother had been horrified when he told her he was joining the police force, the summer after he had graduated from OSU with a degree in criminal justice.

"I thought you were going on to law school!" she had said, collapsing into a kitchen chair as if shot.

He had sat down across from her. "I think I can make a bigger difference as a cop."

"You could be a prosecutor. A judge. A senator."

He shook his head at that. She had hinted before that she had political aspirations for him, but he had none for himself. "By the time you're prosecuting a crime, it's too late. A criminal at that level is unlikely to be saved. It's a done deal. He's a criminal, he's in the life, and he'll almost certainly offend again. If I can get to kids somehow, kids just getting into trouble, steer them away—"

"Then why not be a social worker? At least they don't get shot at!"

They probably did. But he didn't make that point. He addressed the one he thought was important. "You don't have to worry about me, Mom."

"I do have to worry. I'm your mother! It's my job to worry!"

He had thought she was a little crazy to say that, but now that he was a parent himself, he understood it better. The worry came with the love, whether you wanted to worry or not.

* * *

His mother was off on a tour of Australia right now with her boyfriend, half a world away. These days, he thought maybe he should have taken her advice about law school. After a decade of failing to do a fraction of what he had hoped when he became a peace officer, he was, he knew, burning out on the job.

As he pulled up to Aunt Sherryl's house, he got out his phone and typed in, "Mom—hope you're having a great time. Love you," and scheduled it to send at 5:00 this afternoon his time. If he had his time zones right, she'd be getting up about then.

When he looked up, he saw that Sherryl was already out front, fiddling with something in her front flower bed. She finished and stood, waving to him. She looked little like his mother, though only eighteen months separated the two women's birthdays. While they had roughly the same build, short and square-shouldered, they had entirely different faces. Sherryl's long nose and thin lips gave her a hawk-like appearance—or bald eagle, now that her hair had turned entirely white.

It was the kind of thing you could say to her, and she'd not take offense. She could laugh at herself. He liked that about her. Since he had moved here, she'd become a second mother to him, and the other grandmother to Holly.

As she got in the car, he said, "How's my favorite aunt?"

"And how many aunts do you have?"

"One, but she's a winner." He waited while she put on her seatbelt. "Donuts? Denny's? What's your pleasure, ma'am?"

"Fritch's. I'm in the mood for a biscuit, and I like theirs."

They arrived at the restaurant after the worst of the breakfast rush and were seated without a wait.

Their server was Belle, who recognized him. "What'll you have, Officer Friendly?"

"That takes me back." He had done the Officer Friendly gig a few years back in the schools. Probably that hadn't done any lasting good there, either. "Decaf for me."

"Iced tea, please," said his aunt. "No sugar."

When Belle had gone to get their drinks, he said, "How's Jim?"

"He has his good days and bad."

"And you're holding up okay?"

"I'm good," she said. "Loving the spring, getting out in the garden again."

"I mean with Jim."

"I knew what you meant," she said with a smile. "I'm fine, really. How's work?"

He waggled his hand—*comme ci comme ça.*

"Problems? New boss okay?"

"She's fine." She wasn't, but Greg wouldn't complain about that aloud—not even to Aunt Sherryl. He was hoping it'd work itself out. But it was one more straw on the camel's back that was his dissatisfaction with work.

Sherryl said, "You don't look happy."

"I'm fine. Work's okay."

"Uh-huh," she said, clearly not believing him. Belle came with the drinks and his aunt thanked her, and they both gave their orders. Sherryl took the spoon out of her tea and sipped. "You know your mother never wanted you to join the force."

"Funny, I was just thinking about that. About the day I told her I was."

"She quit speaking to me for days when she learned I'd told you about the posting here. For almost a month, she didn't return my calls."

He shook his head. "I didn't know that."

"Oh, it passed. You know your mother."

"I do." He finished his coffee and set the cup at the outer edge of the table, hoping for a quick refill.

"So what's up with work?"

"It's just—I don't know. It's the system, you know, a whole messed up system, this ugly machine, clanking along, and I feel like I'm a little cog in it, contributing somehow to the mess.

That's not why I decided to do the work. I want to make things better, somehow."

"You're what—thirty now?"

"Thirty-two. And you're suggesting that's too old to be such an idealist?"

She shook her head. "Not at all. Idealism is nice. I was wondering more about a career change. You're plenty young enough for that, still. That's why I asked."

"Enough about me. I'm just tired after the shift, full of complaints. Let's talk about you."

She let him change the subject. "I'm boring. Gardening in the mornings. Nursing home every day, TV most nights, mah-jongg once a week, gardening club once a month. Nothing is ever new with old people, except new health complaints, and I don't have much to complain about there. Now tell me about that sweet girl of yours. Hard to believe she's almost done with second grade."

And for the rest of the meal they talked about Holly, and spring, and nothing at all serious.

* * *

His cell phone rang as he locked the front door after himself. He was desperate for some sleep, but he checked the number.

Kimberly. His ex. Oh man, that woman's awful timing. Or did she do this on purpose?

Sighing, he thumbed on the phone. "Hi," he said.

"Let me talk to Holly," his ex-wife said.

"It's nearly ten here. She's in school."

Silence. Then, "I don't know why you won't let her have a cell phone. I can afford it."

"If she had a cell," he said with exaggerated patience, "she couldn't answer it in class anyway."

"Still—"

"Look, Kim," he said, "I have to get some sleep. Let's fight later. Or, here's an idea—you can call your daughter tonight, any time between five and eight."

"I'll be busy," she said, and the phone went dead.

He turned off the phone and said to it, "Selfish witch," but without any heat. Mostly, Kim just tired him out. Her attention to Holly was sporadic, at best. He had given up child support in exchange for primary custody, and he had soon suspected he could have had custody without giving up anything. Well, it is what it is, as they say. His disappointment in his ex was manageable. It was Holly he felt bad for.

He unbuttoned his shirt and, once he hit his bedroom, dropped it to the floor as he kicked off his shoes. He should toss his uniforms shirt in the laundry, but he was too tired to do it now. He unbuttoned his jeans and slipped on his sleep mask to shut out the daylight seeping in around the blinds—and was asleep as soon as his head sank into the pillow.

* * *

Sherryl waved to her nephew as he drove off and stood on the sidewalk, telling herself not to worry about him. It was normal, she thought, to question your career choices about his age. He was bright, and he'd work through it.

She glanced up at the sky, assessing the few clouds moving lazily to the east. The forecast this morning had promised rain, probably thunderstorms in the afternoon, so she didn't need to water the garden now.

She wished she could spend all morning puttering around, planting some annual seeds, at least. She had impatiens, morning glory, and coleus seeds, saved or exchanged for at the garden club. She could tie off the fading tulips, dig some compost into the vegetable patch, readying it for the peas and spinach and green beans.

But that would have to wait until she visited Jim. She'd take him some of the daffodils from the side border. He'd probably not notice them—truth be told, he probably wouldn't have noticed until she mentioned it even before the Alzheimer's—but she'd feel slightly better for brightening up his room.

Sometimes, dealing with Jim's troubles, that was the best she could expect, making herself feel slightly less guilty. She cut her daffodil bouquet last thing before hopping in the car and driving to the nursing home.

Edgewood Manor Care Facility was on the southwest side of town, a few blocks south of the high school. The first night he had been put in there—no, be honest, that *she* had put him in there—a Friday in November, she had leaned her head against the glass of his one window and heard the distant cheers from the football game. She had stayed up in a chair, watching him until he fell asleep that night, fully realizing only as she got up to leave him that they'd never sleep in the same bed again.

So many little heartbreaks came in a lifetime. The more Jim slipped away from her, the more there would be.

Today, as she walked across the home's parking lot, there was no sound but the occasional swish of tires on the quiet side street and a raucous cardinal calling out his territorial rights from a pin oak on the front lawn. The air was thick with humidity, and by the time she was opening the front door, she was tacky with perspiration.

The receptionist, familiar with Sherryl's daily visits, barely glanced at her as she walked through the lobby. Sherryl took the first left turn, right again through double doors, which were locked at night, past an old woman leaning on a walker in her doorway, querulously disagreeing with a nurse, and went almost all the way down the hall.

She paused at the door to his room took a deep breath to gather herself, and strode in. "Good morning, dear," she said cheerfully, moving to drop a kiss on his cheek. "It's Sherryl." He looked at her blankly. "Your wife," she said in a softer tone.

"I know that," he said, frowning at her as if she were the one with brain problems.

"I brought you some flowers from our garden. You remember when we planted all the bulbs that one fall—what was it, eight years ago? You tilled, I planted."

"Because I kept planting them upside down," he said.

"That's right." She felt her smile relax, become real. "I made you stick to digging after that."

"Pointy ends up," he said.

She nodded. "Just so." She showed him the flowers again. "I'm going to put these in water for you, okay?"

She had turned to the dresser that held the vase when he said, "Sherryl?"

"Yes, my love?" She turned her head toward him.

"When did you get so old?"

Her breath caught. "I don't know, Jim. I wonder that myself every time I look in the mirror." She turned her back on him. "I'll be right back."

She went into the private bathroom, shut the door without locking it, and stared at her face in the mirror. He was right—she *was* old. In his mind, he must think of her at a different age, perhaps thirty-three, when they met, three years after her divorce when she was certain she'd never remarry. Hell, in the years between Richard and Jim, she hadn't even let a man stay overnight. Or maybe Jim saw her at forty, or at fifty. Of course, she often thought of herself as that young—or younger.

Do people change all that much between eighteen and eighty? Some days, she thought not. Oh sure, you learn more. And as your sex hormones fade, you quit acting so stupidly to attract people, and you gain patience.

And you can get sick.

Like Jim, you can get the worst kind of sick.

Or maybe not the worst—there were diseases even more awful than Alzheimer's—but bad enough. He still had some good days among the bad days. She wondered which it would be today.

"And for which of us do you mean?" she asked her reflection. Truth was, his good days—the days when he knew where and when he was—were good days for her, but bad ones for him. He hated being like this, and when he had those "good" days, he understood what he had become. So they were bad days for him.

"Quit being selfish," she said to herself, and she set about arranging the flowers for the room where her husband was going to die. Not today—maybe no time soon—but one day.

* * *

Malika Landers took a deep breath, told her heart to quit beating so fast, and looked out over the classroom of fellow seniors.

Imagine them naked.

Eww. No, that wouldn't work. Who came up with that awful advice?

She squared her shoulders and began. "The principle reasons behind the Spanish-American War." Her title. The slackers in the back row fidgeted. Losers. They were going nowhere. She pushed her gaze to the front row, where the good students waited for her to go on.

"Four contributing factors brought the United States into the war in 1898," she said, not even glancing at her notes. She went on, occasionally shifting her gaze to Mr. Shimmer, the history teacher. She had to begin glancing at her notes as she got past the introduction she'd memorized, but she kept her back straight and maintained eye contact with her audience most of the time.

Vary your timbre.

She felt inside for the rhythms she had taken in from years of listening to a great preacher, toned them down by about half, and finished her speech, only a minute over the assigned time. Sarah Milligan, in the first row, gave an approving nod.

Mr. Shimmer stood and said, "Excellent work, as always,

Malika. Who's next?"

Sarah's hand shot up, as did Jake Bradley's. Jake wasn't good in some classes, but he loved history and, along with Malika and Sarah, set the curve for the class. Unlike Sarah and Malika, he didn't care at all that he did.

I can't dislike Sarah, because she's too nice, but I'd sure like to beat her out in class ranking. And Jake's not my competition anywhere but here.

She listened to Jake's presentation on the anti-war movement of the end of the 19th century. His speech had—what would you call it?—*scope*, that's the word, Malika thought. He connected things well, reached out to religion and politics and back in time to the Civil War, connected the women's suffrage movement and the continuing fight of blacks in the South for equality, and painted a big picture, like a mural, of his topic.

I'm only painting little landscapes. I must learn to expand my scope like this, if I'm going to shine at Kenyon next year.

At the end of the class, Malika stopped to congratulate Jake on a good presentation. He mumbled his thanks and hurried away.

Sarah came over. "Poor shy bastard," she said. "He likes his females safely in history books."

Malika grinned at that insight. "Coming to debate?"

"Of course. Gotta practice whupping you."

They walked out of the classroom together. At the corner of the courtyard, they separated to go to different classes. Turning toward her trig class, Malika felt a hand touch her elbow. When a slight tug didn't dislodge it, she turned to see who it was.

It was Adam, his guitar case slung over his shoulder. "Heya, Meek."

"I can't be late to class."

"I'll walk you there," he said.

She couldn't stop him from walking any direction he pleased, so she turned down the hall and he fell in beside her. "How's school?"

"Good, and you?"

"I'm doing okay."

"Still planning on going up to UT?"

"Probably just commute over to the community college for my first two years, now. It's not that important to me where I get my schooling."

"It should be."

"I know you think that, Meek. I can't afford four straight years anyway, so I don't think it matters where I do my first, you know? I'll have to stop and work at some point anyway."

She did know. "I'm lucky to have the scholarship."

"Luck had no part in it. You've worked your ass off."

She didn't argue, just made her voice bright as she said, "So, here's my class. See you—"

"Would you go out with me on Friday? A movie, maybe? Just as friends."

She looked at him, finally meeting his eyes, and shook her head slowly.

He lowered his voice to almost a whisper. "I miss you."

"I have to work anyway," she said. "Mr. Duncan is on nights this week."

"Would you if he wasn't?"

"*Weren't.* It's the conditional mood you need after an 'if.'"

"I know why you do that. Correct my grammar."

"It's to improve your speech. I'm trying to be helpful."

"No you aren't. You're trying—" He waved it off. "Look, Malika—"

"I have to get to class. The bell's about to ring."

"What if I call you? Tonight. At Mr. D's."

"I have to go." She turned for the door.

"Damn it, Meek," Adam said.

She kept walking away from the pleading note in his voice.

And cursed him as she struggled all period to keep her mind on cosecants.

Captain T

We're in Bloomington, amid more hot-hot-hot college girls, and wait—you hear that? That, my friends, is a storm siren. A line of squalls is sweeping east-northeast, right across southern Indiana. Let me show you the radar on my laptop—zoom in on it, Felix. Here's the yellow quadrilateral right where we are. Tornado watch. And—let me click in—there's a patch of nasty high-top storm coming right our way, in red on the screen. I'm firing up our Doppler just as soon as I upload this vid, and we'll be down for the chase. It's just about 10:30 here, but unseasonably warm for April, and I wouldn't be surprised to see this cell spin out a couple of EF1s before noon. And there are more squalls stacked up right behind it too.

Awesome, right? If you're in the storm area, pay attention to the warnings and take shelter. Me and Felix won't, though. We'll be Captain T and his faithful sidekick, chasing down the storms, bringing you live video. Catch you on the dryline.

Chapter 2

An irksome beeping dragged Greg out of sleep. What the hell? Had he set his alarm for the wrong time? He felt for the snooze button, but pushing it didn't stop the beeping. Tearing his eye mask off, he looked around. That wasn't his ring tone, either.

Beep...beep...beep. "This is the National Weather Service. There is a severe storm warning in effect for the Ohio counties of Preble, Montgomery, Clark, and Greene."

The NOAA radio, the weather radio that he had stashed under the bed.

"At this time, a line of tornado-producing thunderstorms is progressing east-northeast through southern Indiana, producing hail up to 2 inches and spawning three tornados thus far. The leading edge of rain will cross into Ohio before 2:00 this afternoon, local time. Persons in these areas should be on the lookout soon thereafter for threatening weather conditions and listen for later statements and likely warnings."

He looked at his clock. 12:38. Less than three hours of sleep, not nearly enough. But he needed to check out the alert. Bad enough storms, and he might get called into work.

Greg stumbled into the living room and hunted for the TV remote, having no success. Who'd had it last? Right, Holly. That meant it could be anywhere. Might even be with her, at school, in her backpack. He kneeled on the floor and looked under furniture, saw a fruit roll-up wrapper and a stray piece of popcorn under the sofa, grabbed them up to throw away, but still no remote. Giving up, he punched on the box to turn on the TV and tried the Weather Channel, but they had total bullshit programming on.

He changed to the other weather channel, the one he could never remember the name of, and lucked out. They had the local weather on. Radar showed a line of storms stretching across Indiana. Not into Ohio yet.

When the newsreader came back on, she immediately threw the broadcast over to a tornado expert sitting at a desk. He introduced a video segment of about 40 seconds, showing a skinny twister snaking along open farmland and then lifting, lying on its side, and getting sucked back into a black cloud.

"No apparent damage from that one," he said, "and probably it was no worse than an EF1, but there will be more tornados today, and very likely much stronger ones as the day progresses." He showed a map that stretched from southeastern Illinois to Pittsburgh, with the current radar in greens, yellows and, here and there, blotches of red. The radar flashed off, to be replaced with a yellow parallelogram and a time stamp. "These are the times you can expect to be under a tornado watch." The parallelogram stuttered east across the country, starting at the Illinois-Indiana border and moving east-northeast.

The graphic ran again, half-speed, and Greg could see Fidelity under the yellow zone in two graphics—2:00-3:00 and 3:00-4:00.

Holly would be getting out of school at 3:15. The elementary school was quite old and had a basement. A lot of newer schools did not have basements. She was probably safer there than she would be at home—but he knew he'd still feel the pull to be with her if anything went wrong.

But he might be called into work, which meant he wouldn't

have the option of being with his daughter. He had only 90 minutes to get ready either way, in case the worst happened. No more sleep for him.

He suspected that the dispatcher would call before too long. And there were no clean uniforms.

Leaving the TV on, he went to collect laundry, setting everything on the short cycle, on warm, remembering at the last second to take his badge off and check his pockets for pens.

He poured this morning's coffee down the sink and made himself a new pot, one and a half normal strength. His brain wasn't hitting on all cylinders yet, and caffeine would help—not as much as sleep, but a little.

If the storms got bad, his adrenaline would keep him alert. But for now he'd have to rely on coffee. And he'd better make himself a sandwich too. No telling if he'd have a chance to eat supper.

* * *

Malika pushed her plate away, still hungry, but unwilling to finish the sweet potato "tots" which were fine when warm but, when cooled, congealed into.... She picked one up on her fork. "What's a poetic term for this?" she asked her debate partner, Dylan.

"Pomme a la graise," he said.

She put down the rejected tot. "Why do people think French means poetic? Or classy?"

"Interesting matter for debate, but not *our* debate, which is still, as it has been all spring, term limits. Do you have any more rebuttals for the pork barrel argument? You know Cody will pound on that again, given any opportunity."

She tried to focus on the debate. "First, change the term we're using—impossible to defend anything with the term 'pork' or 'pig' in it—which is probably altogether unfair to pigs, but what can a pig-lover do?"

Dylan steered her back on track. "To?"

LOU CADLE

"District-specific projects, ones that stimulate the economy, provide jobs, yadayadayada."

"Have anything new in one of those yadas?"

"A person local to the area would know best—"

"Old."

"And since everybody does it—"

"No."

"Over time, it comes out even and fair to all Americans—"

"Also not new."

"Give me a second. I'm thinking." She pushed her plate away. Truth to tell, she was distracted by thoughts of her personal life again, and hating herself for it. She had to focus on school. There was still time—six weeks—to improve her class ranking, and a shot at the top three in class rank. "Maybe I'd think better with dessert in me."

Dylan glanced at his watch. "You don't have the time."

"Rats. Dylan, we'll do fine in the debate, and I'll try to come up with something new—or at least a new way to say something old—before 3:30. I promise."

"It'll have to do, I suppose."

She gave him a look, and, as he walked away, she muttered, "Bossy," under her breath.

"Takes one to know one," he shot back over his shoulder.

She strapped on her backpack, gathered her tray, and walked to the trash cans. When she caught herself scanning the corner of the cafeteria where the musicians hung out, looking for blond hair and Adam's height, she silently cursed herself. Scraping the food into the trash barrel, she muttered, "It's just hormones."

A short, pimply underclassman snorted and then blushed when she looked directly at him. He scurried away, the back of his neck apple-red.

Good God, was she ever that young?

* * *

20

Sherryl turned the page of the novel—the new Steve Hamilton, from the library—that she was reading aloud to Jim, and finished the chapter. Tucking in a bookmark, she closed it, put it in her bag, and then closed her eyes, rolling her head to ease the tension in her neck.

"Sherryl," Jim said. "When did you get here?"

She opened her eyes and met his gaze. He looked, somehow, more *there*. "A bit ago, Jim."

"You should have woken me up."

No sense in explaining to him that she'd been here for more than an hour. It'd only make him feel bad. "I will next time."

"I don't know how many times we have left, love. I think I'm losing myself. Am I? Is it bad?"

"You're doing fine, Jim." She reached out and brushed his cheek, feeling the texture of the white whiskers. "Except you could stand a shave."

"You know what I mean."

"I know."

His eyes changed, just like that, a two-second fade. "I think your mother was here earlier."

Her mother had been dead twelve years.

"Everyone cares about you and visits." His brother had driven down once in the past three months, her sister had driven over twice from Columbus, and Greg came by every couple weeks, though she knew that from the nurses and not Greg himself. And her? She was here every day, without fail, except one day that she had worried she was coming down with the flu and didn't want to spread it among these frail old bodies. It wasn't much, but Jim got more visitors than a lot of these other old people had.

Jim said, "I'm hungry. Is it time for breakfast?"

"We just had lunch." But he hadn't eaten much, and he seldom did. He was a bag of bones now. "You feel like dessert?"

He nodded. "Pie. Rhubarb pie."

"We'll see what they have."

"I think we should take another cruise line next time. The buffet here isn't the best. And they never serve their pie warm. Damned boat. We paid them good money, didn't we?"

"Yep. You're right about that."

"Remind me to complain to the steward tonight."

"After we go dancing," she said, entering into his fantasy with him. The nurses said to keep them grounded to reality, but Sherryl wondered, to what end? What could it hurt to be on a cruise ship? "You want to dance?"

"That'd be nice." His eyes drifted shut. "I like slow dancing with you. Always gets me horny."

She laughed, remembering. It had, back in the day. "I love you so much, Jimmy."

But he was asleep.

Captain T

We got our first twister today on film, uploaded and on the site, which you should check out, and I have a good feeling about getting more. That first one finished about as fast as Felix does in the sack, right, bro? Just kidding, ladies, he's a love machine—not that I'd know from personal experience. That's as rumor has it.

Anyway, we're south of Indie right now, mobile Doppler on, trying to keep to the south side of that deep red, on the lookout for a telltale hook echo. The big city is getting rain, but looks like they'll miss out on twister fun today—they're going to be spinning up twenty miles south of the city limits, at the closest.

There's a lot of rain-wrap right now so we're using a bit of caution, making sure we have a southern escape route open if we need it. But we're not chickening out—I'd like to grab some shots of tornadogenesis today for you. There's nothing more thrilling than watching the tornado come out of nowhere, that first thin hint, the debris field spinning up, making it visible. It's poetry in motion, don't you think?

Time to remind you about our sponsor for today's chase. Tires, ladies and gentlemen—reliable tires are crucial to us when we chase a massive tornado and just as important to you....

Chapter 3

Greg's cell rang at 2:02, just as he was cleaning up after lunch. He dried his hands and picked up the phone. "Duncan," he answered it.

"Greg, it's Rosemary." The new chief, Rosemary Stephens.

"And you want me to come in."

"I need you to, yes."

"I've been watching the weather on the boob tube. When do you want me?"

"Asap," she said. "I'll put you on patrol, doubled up. I have you in Massey's car to start with."

Darrell Massey—old, scrawny, getting lazy, and surprisingly mean when he felt insulted. Not the best cop on the force, not the worst. He was getting near retirement and happy about it. Greg walked to the dryer to check it—still fifteen minutes to go. "Okay. He can swing by the station and pick me up. I'll be there in twenty."

"Make it sooner."

"If I can." He'd put on a damp shirt, if need be. "I may need to leave for fifteen minutes this afternoon when school lets out to get my daughter to daycare."

He heard her move the phone away briefly, to sigh, before she said goodbye. She didn't have children of her own and didn't have much sympathy for family issues. Well, screw it. He was coming in when he should be sleeping, so she could adjust for him too.

Outside, a light rain was pattering against the window, making a pleasant sound. But the television, which he could still hear from the kitchen, was still saying worse was coming. Much worse.

He opened the dryer. Clothes were still damp—too damned humid today for them to dry quickly. He grabbed a damp uniform shirt, pinned on the badge, and turned the dryer back on. As he went to shut off the TV, he could hear distant thunder rumbling to the west.

* * *

Twenty minutes later he was punching in the code to the police station's steel back door. Tucking in his shirt, which still wasn't dry, he made his way to Chief Stephens' office. She held up a finger and continued talking—to no one.

Then he realized she was on a conference call. "So we'll do that," the voice came from the phone on her desk. Greg recognized the fire chief's voice. "And I doubt we'll have a chance to talk for the next two hours. It'll get busy soon."

"Stay safe," she said.

"You too," the fire chief said, and he was gone.

"Anything new?" Greg asked.

"Unconfirmed tornado touched down in Union County, Indiana."

That was just across the border. "Is it headed our way?"

"That, I don't know. But if it *is* still on the ground, we may be in its path."

"Do they know how fast it's moving?"

"Surely someone does, but I haven't heard."

"How strong is it?"

She shook her head. "Been too busy to look it up. I'll have

Grace do all that in a second."

"So what do you want us to do out there on the street?"

"I want most of you mobile. You and Massey have the southwest corner of town, Higgins and Genoa the northwest corner. Don't worry about crossing out of town limits—I've cleared that with the sheriff—and keep your eye out for tornados."

"Don't we have a storm watch network? Radar?"

"All that. But I want troops on the ground, ready to respond the instant something goes wrong. Stay out of its way, of course. I want you *on* the ground, not in it." She smiled at her own quip.

Greg didn't. "Remember, I may have to get my daughter soon."

"Isn't there anyone else who can do that for you? You have family in town, right?"

"My aunt—she's probably still at the nursing home. Her husband is ill."

"A babysitter?"

"She's a high school student, and she's never available until after 4:00, and I think not even that today. She can pick up Holly from daycare at five every...." He trailed off, seeing her lack of interest in his child care arrangements. "I'll stay on my personal phone about it and try to get something else arranged."

"That'd be best."

"But if I can't, I'm coming back to pick her up at school."

"Where's her mother, again?"

"Atlanta, Georgia—a little far to make it in time for the final bell at Central Elementary." He was losing his patience—and he shouldn't.

She made an irritated face. "Okay. Get going."

"Yes, ma'am," he said, leaving. He hesitated in the hallway to check his weapon. Ready to go.

He made his way to the front desk and checked on Massey's ETA—"turning in to the parking lot right now," said their office manager. As he turned to go, she said, "Make sure there're two helmets in the trunk of the patrol car before you leave the station."

"Thanks, Grace. Will do."

He went through to the back door and held a hand up at the prowl car edging along. It came to a stop and he opened the passenger door and leaned in. "Pop the trunk, would you?"

"Why?"

"To check gear."

"It's fine."

"Fine enough for two?" As they patrolled singly, usually they didn't need to keep gear for two.

The trunk release snapped. As Greg made his way back, the rain intensified. He dug through the trunk and found two helmets, one riot shield, one respirator, two ripstop vests. Enough for the day's needs, he thought.

He slipped into the car, running his hand over his head to squeeze some of the rain off.

"Startin' to come down now," Massey said.

"Yeah." Greg wiped his hand on his pants leg. "Chief says to patrol the southwest of town."

"I heard." His tone was clipped.

"Why's everybody in a rotten mood today?"

"Low barometric pressure. Makes everybody short-tempered. At least my wife says it does."

"How is she?"

"Same old."

"Kids?"

"Don't hear from them very often. You know Trent's in Guatemala, with the oil company." Massey steered out into the street and came to stop at one of the dozen traffic lights in town. "How's your kid?"

"Light of my life."

"Yeah, when they're young, they are. And she's a girl—that

helps too. If we'd had girls, I bet at least one would have stayed nearby."

"At least your boys aren't in the path of the storm today. I may have to go back and pick up Holly at 3:15 when school lets out if I can't find someone else to do it."

They both glanced at the clock on the dash. 2:34. "Remind me," said Massey.

The car turned, and they were headed west, one block south of Main.

On the horizon, a vast black cloud stretched across the sky. Lightning flashed underneath it, half obscured by the rain. The brightness danced across the cloud bottoms hanging over the farmland.

Massey said, "One thousand one, one thousand two." When he reached fifteen, he gave up. There was no thunder. "Still some miles off," he said.

"I wonder how fast it's coming," Greg said.

"Fast enough," said Massey.

"Yeah," said Greg, wondering not for the first time why people said such nonsensical things. Just to fill the air with noise, he supposed. "I gotta get on my phone and make arrangements for Holly if I can, if that's okay."

"Don't mind me," said Massey, driving toward the heart of the storm.

Greg could feel the wind picking up—straight winds, blowing almost right toward them, whistling into the cracks in the windows.

He dialed the elementary school.

* * *

At the nursing home, Sherryl was listening to Jim's neighbor, sitting in a wheelchair, blocking the door, talking about cousins and second cousins who Sherryl didn't know and couldn't care a fig about.

"That's nice," she said, when the woman finally took a breath. "But I'm visiting my husband today. Maybe we can talk another day."

"And then she said," the old lady went on, wheezing a little as she tried to get the story out quickly with insufficient lung capacity.

The wheelchair motor ground, and its bumpers thumped against the door jamb.

"What's that?" Jim said, waking.

She rested her hand on his arm.

"Where am I?" he said. "What's that noise?"

Sherryl went to the door to see if the door could close, but the old lady's legs stuck into the room. Sherryl put her hand on the door jamb to lean out over the woman and look for staff to take the lady back to the room—and hopped back when the old woman kicked her. Her foot was slippered, so it didn't hurt, but still.

"You're not listening!" the woman said, red-faced with anger.

"I'm listening," she said.

"You're a liar. Just like my brother. He's a liar too. He said I kicked over the milk and I didn't—" And she was off again, complaining about unfair treatment that reached back into the Eisenhower era, whining over spilled milk, literally. Sherryl wondered if she'd ever let up, or if this old complaint had been circling in her mind for that long. The things we waste energy on.

Sherryl leaned forward again to see down the hall, hoping to wave a staff member over, and this time the old woman reached up and pinched her right breast—hard.

"Damn," Sherryl said, slapping the crabbed hand away. That hurt! Then she shouted, "Hey, can I get some help down here?" They didn't want the nurse call button to be used except in an emergency, but she was about thirty seconds from using the button anyway.

"Just like my brother, just like my brother," the old woman began to chant.

"If your brother had breasts like mine, I'd be surprised," Sherryl told her. Then louder, "Hey, some help?"

Finally, an orderly came from down the hall. Sherryl pointed at the woman and said, "Maybe get her back to her room before she bruises me again?"

"C'mon, Mrs. Bronsen," said the orderly to the still-chanting woman. "Cake."

"Cake?" The old lady let go of her brother mantra and perked up.

"Let's go," he said and steered the woman away.

Sherryl closed the door after them. Ack, old people. She hadn't liked children when she was a child, and now that she was an old person, she didn't want to be in this group, either. She'd rather have been born 35 and died that way—but still have gotten her 65 years in.

Jim was fussing with his sheet. He pointed at her and said, as if continuing a conversation they'd been having all along, "And all they talk about is Kim Kardashian anyway."

"Ain't that the truth," Sherryl said.

Outside, a rumble of thunder sounded in the distance.

"Getting darker out there," said Sherryl, going to the window. The clouds must be thick to cut out so much light, and wind was whipping through the spring leaves on the trees.

"Is she out there?"

"Kim Kardashian?" she asked him, staring at the sky. It looked nasty.

"My wife!" he said, irritated at her obtuseness.

"I'll keep an eye out," she said. "I'm sure she'll be back any second." She rubbed her right breast where the old claws had pinched it. Her breast was going to be purple by tonight. She bruised so easily these days. Old age was such a delight.

She was studying the dark clouds when her cell phone rang.

* * *

Malika passed the sheet music up through the altos who passed it on to the student chorus assistant. She checked the wall clock and saw that she had twelve minutes to pee and get to debate club. She wanted to wash her face too—it had been so muggy today, she felt like a walking Crisco can.

She draped her pack strap over her forearm and left the choral room, following a tall white girl in a skirt and high heels that click-click-clicked on the tile floor.

Outside, Adam was waiting. For her?

Yes, for her.

She motioned him back from the flow of students heading for the door, back toward the band practice rooms. "Don't you have jazz band now?"

"Yeah. We're on a break."

"I have debate." She made a point of looking around for a clock, even though she knew the time.

"I just wanted to talk to you. You never said no."

"I said I was working. But yes, that meant no."

"I don't get it. It's just a movie. Or if you want, something else. Saturday morning is good too. We can take a walk. Or I'll take you to the outlet mall, if you want."

"I'm too busy. I want to finish school, Adam. I want to do well in school. I want to ace my last finals."

"Why? You got into Kenyon, you got your scholarship, you have your future all planned out. This last month of our senior year, we're supposed to slack."

"I don't have slacking in me, I suppose. I'm just not a quitter."

He raised his eyebrows, and his look said, *Yeah? You quit us.*

She couldn't deny that. "Gotta go."

"I wish you'd talk to me. You said we could still be friends, and we're not even that, now."

"You're my friend," she said, without meeting his gaze.

31

"No. I'm not." He was following her. "You aren't treating me like a friend. You never did tell me why, Meek. If I'm your friend, don't I at least deserve to know the truth?"

"I did tell you. I'll tell you again in an email later today, if you want. But I have to get to my club."

"Don't bother with writing me some lame excuse," he said. "I deserve better than an email. And I deserve better treatment than this."

She walked away, not trusting herself to look at his face before she left. The truth? She was glad he was angry at her, there was a truth. Anger was easier to deal with than begging. Better than his looking hurt. Anger, she understood. She could stand tough against anger. Anger was like a wall you could punch. His hurt was like mist that you couldn't push against. It just wrapped itself around you and made you feel lost.

She detoured into the only girl's bathroom in the music wing, ending the discussion, and she looked at herself in the mirror there. "I know what I want," she said to herself, to distract herself from feeling bad about Adam. "Top three in class. Graduation. Boys later—maybe in junior or senior year, but maybe only after college. Marriage when I'm established solidly in a profession. Babies, never. Unless I marry a rich man, never." She knew she couldn't have it all. That wasn't possible for girls like her. And she had made her choice. She was going to *be* someone.

"Talking to yourself?" one of the pretty white girls— cheerleader or pep-squad-type—said, exiting a stall, and brushing by her. "You know what that's a sign of."

The door swung shut behind the girl.

"Don't wash your hands or anything," Malika said to the door, then quickly ducked down to check the other stalls. She was alone now. But she was done talking to herself anyway.

She ran the hot water at a trickle for a few seconds to get it warm. She dug in her pack for her own facial soap, wrapped in tissue paper in a zipper plastic bag. She'd never been to the ocean, but the soap smelled like she imagined the sea might. She had it in her hand, sniffing it in pleasure, when, in the distance, the town storm siren went off.

Captain T

It's Captain T again, standing at the state boundary between Indiana and Ohio. It's 3:12 p.m., and what you're looking at right now is not me—obviously—but a front-flank supercell storm, a textbook structure, shot from the south. It's moving east of northeast, at maybe twenty-five miles per hour. You have (camera pans right) the leading edge of the storm, with rain visible beneath. Behind that, I can guess from radar there's a wall cloud, but I sure can't see it. And there's a distinct tail cloud, the only clear feature, visible in the space before the next cell off to the west comes along.

I can see some inflow, but I'm not sure the camera is catching it. And when we drove out of it to take these shots from the south, we hit a strong gust front. I'll pull up a graphic for you on the front page of the website by the next time we post a vid, so you can see a drawing of what's happening in there behind all this rain.

Somewhere up in that dark area, we have vertical rotation, and we have all the ingredients for tornadogenesis. I'm taking over driving duties to get us closer, so Felix can film out the window as we approach the storm, and I'm saying a 60 percent chance of tornadogenesis.

Everything looks perfect. Doppler is right. Pressure, wind sheer, it's all right on the money. The only problem I see is, if we get a twister and go in, I think it may be rain-wrapped. It's an HP—that's high precipitation—cell. We may not be able to get good shots for you. And that also means that the people ahead of it may not see it coming.

So we'll get as close as we can—and we'll see what we can see.

Chapter 4

"What's that noise?" said Jim.

"It's my phone," Sherryl said.

"That's not a phone. A phone sounds like—ring, ring. *A phone.*"

She dug her cell out, while Jim tried to imitate a 1965 Bell phone. "Hello?"

"Aunt Sherryl, it's Greg. I'm at work and I need a favor. Are you still at the nursing home?"

"Yes, talking with Jim."

Jim said, "What are you doing?" He looked around the room. "Are you talking to me? Who are you talking to?" His voice was getting whinier.

She said to Greg, "Who has forgotten for a moment what cell phones are."

"Ah, not a great day. I'm sorry."

"He's in and out."

"Okay, don't worry about Holly, then."

She checked the time. "You need someone to pick her up? I could get there by 3:20, 3:30 at the latest."

"Don't worry about it—not just yet, at least. If there's no tornado, I'll get there a few minutes late."

"A tornado? Are we under a warning?"

"Yes, there was a touchdown in Indiana, just over the border, and it may be headed our way. The same storm is coming, at any rate."

"Oh." She wondered if she should do something here—and what.

"So you stay safe. Is there a basement there at the facility?"

"I don't think so, but I'll check."

"Inner room, then, if one comes. Or the bathroom. Just stay away from the windows. Gotta go." And the phone was dead.

She tucked the phone into her jacket pocket, wondering what to do first. She'd like to help with Holly, but her first obligation was here. "Be right back, Jim."

"Is that a phone too?" he said, his face turned toward the window. He was hearing a siren, a fire truck or ambulance moving through the streets a few blocks away.

"No, sweetie," she said, on her way out the door.

Nothing was happening in the hallway, so she kept going to see if they were doing anything to prepare for the storm. In the central area of the home, staff were pulling residents away from the big glass windows, pushing wheelchairs, assisting people in walkers, trying to get them away from all the glass.

Sherryl went to the reception desk. The girl was on the phone. When she hung up, Sherryl said, "Do we know for sure there's a tornado?"

"The TV and radio say there is one."

"My husband can't move easily on his own. He's in room 414. If I can get some help with him?"

"Honestly, ma'am, I don't know when that'll happen. They have to move all these people out here back into the hall and—" She stopped to answer the ringing phone.

"Is there a basement here?"

The girl didn't answer. But it didn't matter. No way could she get Jim all the way to a basement, even if there were one. And she wouldn't leave him on his own.

She trotted back to his room. When she went in, she heard the storm siren start up, low at first, then rising in tone to an insistent shrill. Rain lashed against the window.

"Can you sit up?" she asked Jim, going to his side. "Take my arms, and I'll help you." She reached for his hands and tugged.

He snatched them back. "What are you doing?"

"I want to take a walk with you."

"Where's my rhubarb pie?" He pushed at his covers. "I'm too warm."

She tried to calm herself. Rushing Alzheimer's patients was about the worst possible thing to do if you wanted them to cooperate. They'd usually go along with slow and sweet, but rush them, get them anxious? Forget it. Her voice was probably conveying her worry, making him less inclined to follow instructions.

"I'll raise your bed, and we'll get you into a wheelchair. Wouldn't a little walk be nice?"

"Pie," he said, petulant.

"We'll walk down to the cafeteria, then. Get you some nice pie." She raised his hospital bed, and his blankets fell away.

She turned to get the folding wheelchair—his own, not the home's—tucked against the wall by the dresser. She fumbled getting it open, slammed the footrests down and wheeled the chair over to the bedside.

"Okay, let's see if we can get you in here," she said.

He looked mulish.

Again, she took a deep breath and tried to calm herself. Pretend it doesn't matter. Then he'll do it.

A crack made her jump and look at the window. A branch had gotten torn off a tree and had hit the window. The wind plastered it there. For a second, the green leaves twisted into the shape of an angry face, a jack-o'-lantern leer, then the wind shifted and the branch was carried off. She hurried to the window and looked out, but the rain was coming down so hard, she couldn't see a thing except the sheeting rain.

Back to the wheelchair. She needed someone to help her, because Jim wasn't going to be any help. But there was only her. She needed to at least get him away from the window. The hall would be easier, but the bathroom might be safer.

She pulled the wheelchair out so she could get ahead of it, and pulled it back in after her until the footrests nudged her ankles.

The wind picked up even more, screaming into the window cracks, making her feel like screaming back in frustration as she tried to manhandle Jim to the side of the bed. Her back twanged.

"Jim. Listen. No fooling, I need to get you into this chair."

"I don't want to. Where are you taking me? Where's my wife?"

"I'm your wife. Here, let's get your legs out from that sheet and over the side."

He shoved at her ineffectually, pitiful in his weakness.

"Oh, Jim." She sighed, rested a moment, then yanked his sheets away.

The storm siren cut out at the same time as the lights. The skies were so dark it was like twilight inside the room.

"Am I going blind?" Jim said.

"No, hon. There's just a storm."

"Then we should get down to the cellar."

"Exactly. Here. Help me."

Finally he quit fighting her and she helped him to the edge of the bed. She hooked the wheelchair with the toe of her sneaker and brought it closer.

Her back hurt—she'd probably pulled a muscle—and the pain stabbed as she tried to lift Jim. She almost could—he was that skinny. She dragged him out of bed, but she couldn't fit him and her and the wheelchair in the space *and* turn around.

Then the chair skidded away.

She had forgotten to set the damned brake.

Unable to stop herself, she slid, her husband in her arms, to the floor.

* * *

Greg hung up the phone with his aunt. He called Malika's mom and left a message to phone him, in case she came home from school early, and he warned Ms. Jefferson to get in the basement, in case the tornado made it to town. He was about to call the elementary school again when a gust of wind hit them, so strong it nearly raised the nose of the heavy police cruiser off the ground.

"Whoa," Massey said. "What the hell—" The car dropped back down onto its springs and bounced. Massey braked. A sheet of rain obscured the view out the front windshield. Massey turned the wipers all the way up, but it did no good.

"Maybe pull off onto the shoulder," Greg said.

"You sound like my wife." The other man steered the car to the right, and Greg could feel the gravel of the shoulder underneath the right front tire. He couldn't hear it for the sound of the rain. Massey said, "Man, that's really—"

Something slammed against the windshield and they both flinched. Whatever it was had been brown and flat, but it was gone before Greg's brain could register what it was. He said, "Is this a tornado? Are we coming into it?"

"No. Or if it is, it'd have to be an awful small one."

Greg stared out the windshield. "I guess not—it's just wind coming straight at us, but sheesh."

They sat still and watched through the windows for a half a minute, the wipers speeding back and forth but doing nothing to clear the view.

"I can't see shit," Massey said.

"Me neither."

A pickup truck whipped past them on the right, honking, the

horn sound Dopplering down as he disappeared into the heart of the storm.

"Asshole," said Massey. "I'd like to give him a ticket, driving like that in this storm."

"We're doing no good sitting out here getting rained on. You think we should turn around and get out of this?"

"Where are we? Exactly, I mean."

"I'll check." Greg turned on the map. "There's a crossroad ahead, a quarter-mile ahead. County Road D."

"I think we should turn on it, see if we can get out of this rain."

"I think we should stay off the road, or get creamed by the next crazy truck driver."

"You sound like my wife again."

"Yeah, but I'm not ever having sex with you, Massey."

"Yep, there it is—you just nailed it. The wife trifecta."

Greg didn't want to joke around. He wanted to get back to town. The closer he was to the elementary school, the better he'd feel. He could feel the storm—feel the pressure changing, maybe. Something in his body knew that worse was coming.

"Radio in," said Massey. "I'll drive along the shoulder."

Greg got Dispatch on the radio and gave their location. "Any tornado spotted?"

"The National Weather Service says there's a hook echo, which means a possible tornado."

"They offer a GPS location on that?"

"No. Let me get a screen up with the radar on it, and I'll try to give you a rough location."

The car was inching along. Massey came to a driveway that forced him back onto the road for a few feet, and Greg turned his head, half-expecting someone to plow into them from the rear. No one did.

The dispatcher came on, drawing Greg's focus back to the radio. "I don't know. I have the radar, I have the streets superimposed. It's dark red where you are—"

"No shit," muttered Massey.

"—but I don't see a hook myself, nothing like a comma or a 'c.' Not on this view. Maybe they have better equipment there at the National Weather Service. They must know what they're talking about."

Greg said, "Which road is the nearest escape from the red bits on the radar for us? What direction, I mean?"

"Definitely east. Back toward town."

"Okay, because we're seeing nothing here because of rain. Over and out."

Massey had driven into the crossroad, and now backed off it and stopped. "I can't even see the damned stop sign."

"Is the stop sign on this side or the other?"

"We're out of town limits. I can't remember, but I don't see how it matters. No one can see it, wherever it is."

"I guess just gun it. Turn left, and then turn left again at the next mile road."

"Okay. Put your tray tables in upright position."

Greg braced himself against the dash.

Massey put on the gas too much, and the car skidded for a moment before the tires caught. Then he accelerated around the corner and got up to speed.

"Man, I can't see a thing. Slow down."

"Wait. I think the rain is easing up."

It was. The rain was letting up, just a little. The wipers were still going as fast as they could, and for a fraction of a second, Greg could see the nose of their own car. "Maybe we should be on the shoulder again."

"I'm moving at 25. I'll keep going. I think it's clearing in this direction."

The road ahead became visible. A car appeared coming toward them, pulled off, canted to the left but still on the shoulder, its hazard lights blinking. "Should we stop?"

Massey glanced in the rearview mirror as they passed. "He's not signaling us. Just sitting there, waiting it out."

"Look at this stuff all over the ground." As the rain eased more, they could see trash on the ground, branches wrenched off trees, cardboard, plywood, a rooster weathervane. "Wind damage."

Massey said, worried, "Maybe we were at the edge of a twister, you think?"

"No," Greg said. "I don't think it was." Rain bounced off the hood. Then he heard the banging and realized it wasn't rain bouncing but ice. "Hail," he said.

"I see it," muttered Massey.

They drove into the hail, which got denser though stayed the same size. "Just pea-sized," said Greg.

"Bad enough. I wish my car were at home in the garage and not outside the station."

"Your insurance will cover it, right? And it might not hail back at the station." He had to raise his voice to be heard over the noise of the hail banging on the metal roof. It took another half a minute to drive out of the end of it.

"I'm up to 35 now," said Massey.

"The other road might be coming up soon." There was a break in the rain—not a full one, just no hail and light rain for a minute—and a little bit of light was making it through the black clouds.

"There's the road. And a stop sign on our side."

Greg saw something up ahead. "Wait," he said. "Look up there."

"Where?"

"Up ahead, maybe a mile or so. You see that black patch?"

"I'm not sure."

"Keep looking, right at the heart of it. There's a place where the black goes almost down to the ground."

They were parked at the stop sign, leaning forward, both of

them trying to see ahead.

"There!" said Greg. "You see that?"

"I don't know what you're talking about."

"I think maybe there's a tornado in there. In that dense black spot."

"I can't see it. Like a little Wizard of Oz thing, or one of the big suckers?"

"Big, I think. But I can't see it clearly, I just think that some of that dark at ground level is moving debris."

"Should we get closer?"

Greg wasn't thrilled at the idea. "I suppose we should, to make sure of what it is before we call it in and cause a panic. Just be ready to turn tail and run, okay?"

"Radio in again. So they know where to look for the bodies."

"Very funny," Greg said, and got on the radio, giving their car number and location, telling the dispatcher what was up. "If you don't hear from us again, then yeah, it's probably a tornado."

"Radio immediately, would you, once you know? We'll get the storm siren going."

They were driving more slowly now. Patches of heavier rain swept by them—a heavy wash, then very little, and another heavy splattering.

Massey said, "It's like being under the damned sprinkler."

"Wait. Look at that—it *is* moving. There's—"

Just as he said it, there was an explosion in the dark area, bits of something being flung out.

"Oh yeah," said Massey. "That can't be good."

"Is it coming right this way?"

"Near enough," he said, mashing down the accelerator.

"Where are you going? That's the wrong direction!" Greg's heart was thumping painfully in his chest as they sped toward the tornado. Not being in control of the car made the fear worse. His throat felt bone-dry.

"Chill. There's a driveway there to the left. I'm not going to risk getting stuck on the shoulder when I do turn." The next three seconds seemed to fill an eternity, then the car was swinging into the driveway.

Greg kept his eye on the tornado—which still looked nothing like tornados he'd seen on TV. This was just a black patch in the rain, with stuff moving ahead of it, the whirl of debris barely visible through breaks in the sheeting rain. It drew closer, the darkness sweeping over farm fields, a shadow slithering toward them.

Greg felt the car reverse. Then a lurch, and he was thrown against the seat harness.

"Goddamn it!"

Was it the outer edge of the tornado hitting? Were they about to get hurled across the field? Holly's face flashed into Greg's mind. He couldn't look away from the darkness, though.

"Asshole!"

What? He shook off the hypnotic effect of the storm and looked at Massey.

"The bastard hit us!"

Greg turned all the way around to see a short white van behind them. It had come off the road and had clipped the back of the car. Its bumper had caught the fender. He jumped out and ran back, getting soaked again, waving at the driver, who was inching backward.

A young man in the passenger seat leaned out. At the same time as Greg, he said, "There's a tornado!"

Greg walked forward. "Get out of our way," he said, motioning them back onto the road. Only then did he notice the weird round thing on the top of the van. He got to the van window. Beyond the passenger, he saw a deck of electronic equipment, including a radar screen and a graphic of the storm they were in, red and orange in the center, with a dab of white near the center. "No. Wait. What's that?"

"We're storm chasers," the guy said, and he tapped the screen at the heart of the red patch. "That's a rain-wrapped tornado back there. A big one."

Greg glanced back. The thing was still a half-mile away, he could see, now that the paralysis of fear and awe was easing. "Where's it heading?"

The driver said, pointing east, "Straight toward that little town there. It's aimed right toward the crossroads in the middle of it, where the two highways meet. If you're from there, sound the alarm, man."

Then the van pulled away, spraying Greg with gravel as it accelerated onto the road. He ran back to the prowl car. "Get back to town! Go, go!" He yanked the mic from the radio and yelled in the information as he shut the door. He didn't want to yell—he wanted to sound calm and professional, so when people replayed the recording of this later he wouldn't be screaming like an idiot, but his adrenaline was running so high, he couldn't control his voice.

He did manage to give their GPS location, say the tornado was a half-mile southwest of that, and he conveyed the storm chaser's confirmation. Massey hung a right onto the road they'd come out on, and sped up, passing through hail again. Greg said to the dispatcher, "Hit the storm siren, and keep it on."

"Where to?" Massey said, as they approached the crossroads. "Back to the station?"

"Take me to the elementary school," said Greg. "There's a basement there too—you and I can get down there if we need to." It was north of the town center by a half-mile.

"Tell Dispatch that's where we're headed, if you think it's the right move." Massey gunned it. "How long do you think we have?"

Greg twisted around. He couldn't see that ominous black patch. "A few minutes? Until it hits the edge of town, I think." He turned to the radio again and told them it was headed for downtown, where the station was. "You have no more than three minutes to get down to shelter." Dispatch was located underground already—they had been moved there as an anti-terrorist security measure after 9/11—but Grace and Rosemary had to get down there too. He signed off but kept the mic in his hand, in case he thought of something more.

"We could outrun it," Massey said. "If we kept it at fifty or sixty miles an hour, we'd stay ahead of it."

They probably could. Or they could turn north at the next road and drive on out of the line of storms altogether. Greg remembered the radar image on the TV weather station earlier— what? Only an hour ago? East of northeast, the whole thing was in a line, moving that direction. They could, theoretically, go due north or south and escape it. But it was headed for their town and their families and the people they were supposed to protect and serve. All they could really do was run ahead of it and try to get themselves and everyone possible to safety in the seconds remaining.

Especially all those little kids at the elementary school. Especially Holly.

* * *

Malika heard the storm siren—it was just northeast of here, at the town center, and it barely made it through the school's walls. She hadn't been outside all day, hadn't seen a window to the outdoors in more than an hour, so she doubted it could be a serious warning. When did they test it? Maybe it was just the monthly test.

She washed her face, felt better for it, dabbed her soap dry, and put it away in her pack. Then she used the toilet and came back out to wash her hands, for her momma had raised her right.

When she turned the water on, pipes screamed somewhere down the hall. But the scream got louder and louder, until she knew it couldn't be pipes. The floor under her feet began to shake.

A crash made her turn her head toward it, and before she could wonder what the sound was, the outer wall, the wall with the three toilet stalls, came skidding toward her.

It's a dream, she had time to think, and then something fell on her head, and all thinking stopped.

Captain T

We are running like devils, ahead of a tornado, but it's a hard one to see. Rain-wrapped, which means no one in its path will see it coming. We told the authorities, and now we're turning south, a little more than a mile ahead of the storm, to try to get under it. South of it, I mean, behind it. We might get a shot of it that way, and we'll stay safe. We'll follow the thing into this little town which is—what, Felix?—Fidelity, Ohio.

Whoo-ee? Skid a little on the turn, eh? Felix is filming out the window, but I don't imagine you can see a thing more than I can. We'll upload this while we still have access, and I hope to be back with you in a couple minutes with some terrific footage.

Chapter 5

Greg kept an eye on the outside rearview mirror while they pressed onward, but the black cloud wasn't visible now.

"Lights and siren," Massey said, as they whipped past the strip mall at the edge of town.

He slowed down as they hit town, jogged left to avoid the central lights, and wove over to Central Elementary. School was just about to let out—it was 3:13—and as they turned north up Central Street, there was the usual queue of parents in cars picking up their children. The semicircular drive was full, and the line stretched out onto the street.

"Shit," said Massey. "Look at them all. Can't get past."

"Drive up on the lawn. You get out, run along those cars, get the parents inside the building. I'll go inside and have the staff get all the kids downstairs."

"Right."

"And I mean *run*, man. Get yourself safe too."

They left the car's siren and lights on as they both leapt from the car. Let people know it was really an emergency.

He figured he had two or three minutes to get it done. Greg took the front steps in a single leap, shouting to the few parents who walked their kids home, standing under umbrellas, waiting on the stoop. "Get inside."

He slammed through the front doors and grabbed the arm of a sleepy-looking female security guard. "Where's the office?" He couldn't remember.

The woman pointed straight back with her free arm. "What's wrong?"

"Tornado coming. Get everybody down the basement. Start with the closest classrooms to the stairs." Greg ran down the hall she had pointed out and saw the sign for the office. He pushed through the door and said, "Tornado. Sound the alarm. Everybody downstairs."

The receptionist, an older lady, gawped at him. "You have ninety seconds to clear these classrooms," he said. "Where's the principal?"

"In there," she said, indicating an inner office door with her head, and fumbled on an intercom switch.

Greg pushed into the inner office and recognized the principal from a parent's night tour. "Greg Duncan," he said. "There's a tornado coming. On the ground, sighted, no doubt about it. You need to get these kids down to the basement shelter. Now."

The receptionist was speaking with a shaky voice into the intercom.

Greg wanted to run to his daughter's classroom, but he had a job to do first. "You take that side of the building, where your security guard is, and I'll take this. Keep everyone calm, but move 'em out of their rooms and down those stairs quick."

He went back out and motioned the receptionist up. She was repeating her announcement. "Shut that off, and come with me."

She leaned down, and he realized she was fumbling for a purse or something.

"Leave it!" he said. "Let's go!" He held his hand out, and she got up, moving faster than he could have hoped. Lifting a hinged section of countertop, she came with him. "Okay," he said. "There's this wing, that wing, right? One floor, and nobody is anywhere else?"

"There's a music room in the basement on this side, plus the physical plant, storage, supplies. On the other end downstairs, the cafeteria."

"Is anyone in there?"

"I don't...." She shook her head and finally seemed to snap into a higher mental gear. "Not in the cafeteria. But there is a class downstairs in the music room."

"They're fine. Okay, we're going all the way down to the stairwell first. You take this side of the hall, and I'll take the other. Room by room. Get everybody moving. Don't let them pile up. Try not to let anyone fall down the stairs, right?"

"Got it," she said, and trotted along to the last door, which was opening. A few of the doors were, now. Some teachers already had their children lined up and were getting them moving after the intercom announcement.

"Great," said Greg to one, as he passed her. "Not a drill. Get them quickly down to the basement." He went on, flinging open the last door on his side of the hall. It was an art room, empty. He went to the next door and hauled it open. Kids were lining up at a cloakroom niche to get jackets and lunch boxes. "Everybody come up here," he called. "No time for jackets—it'll all be there when you come back upstairs." He hoped that was true. "Double time, now. Quick, quick, who can make it to the door first?"

"No running!" the teacher said.

He went to her and lowered his voice. "You have maybe sixty seconds to get them down. Move them fast." He strode out of that room and went to the next. Those kids were already in the hall, marching down toward the exit sign. Good job, teacher number 3.

The fourth room's children were just exiting as he came to it. He glanced behind himself, saw there was no back-up in the hall. "You're doing great," he said to the first kid. One more room. He opened the door and nearly all the children were lined up at the door except for one, at the back of the class, who the teacher was kneeling by. "Hey kids," he said. "The rest of you can go. Just follow the next class."

One little girl said, "Not without Ms. Henks."

"No, it'll be fine, just this once," he said. "There are plenty of teachers out there. You'll see. Just go out and turn and join the line to the stairs." He had a terrible image of them moving the wrong way. "You know which way the stairs are?" Most of the kids pointed the right direction, and he pointed that way himself. "Exactly. Go downstairs and move forward in the basement hallway as far as you can." He went back to the teacher. "What's wrong?"

"Jerome is a special needs child," she said. "He can't be rushed."

Well, screw that. Greg reached over and hauled up the kid, who immediately began to kick and punch him.

"You shouldn't do that!" she said. "You have to let him take his own time."

"Then we'll leave him to die," he said. "There's a tornado coming, and it'll be here any second. Jerome," he said, lowering his voice to bass tones. "Quit being bad. Shape up, or you—" He tried to think of something the kid would understand. Death likely wasn't it. "Or you won't get any dessert for a week," he said.

The kid began to cry.

Greg said, "Stand up and walk like a big boy. Can you do that?"

"I am big boy," the child said, his lower lip stuck out.

"Prove it," Greg said, carrying him to the door and setting him down gently. "Walk nicely with Ms.—" He looked at the woman.

"Henks," she said, reaching for Jerome's hand.

"And get into the basement," Greg said. Outside the windows, the hail was falling. If nothing had changed about the storm's structure, that meant the tornado wasn't far behind.

The school bell rang for the end of the day. They were out of time.

"Get!" he said to the teacher, who looked upset with Greg. Good God, lady, coddle him later. Now save him.

He went into the hallway, where two dozen children were still lined up in the hall, waiting their turns to go downstairs. The school receptionist was standing there, looking worried.

Greg strode to her. "Good job."

"Are we out of time?"

He nodded, pushed forward and looked down the stairway. Everyone was in one line, sticking to the right of the staircase. "Two lines now," he said, tugging a child over to the left side of the hall. "Go side by side." He motioned the receptionist forward. "You start the second line." The teacher with the problem child was making her way along the hall. "Follow this nice lady here," he said to one girl, taking her hand and leading her over to follow the receptionist down. The kids were so trained to use the right side of stairs, they were reluctant to move to the left. "Hold on to the railing."

The last teacher and her problem child had stopped. For a moment he dithered, then he ran back, snatched the child up and ran him back to the stairs, running down until they hit the back of the line, now halfway down the stairs.

Ahead of him, someone started to scream. He put down the child and pushed between the two lines, trying to get to the noise to stop a panic from spreading. Along the wall, he saw it was a teacher—or at least some adult, her hands over her face, screaming plenty loud despite her mouth being blocked. In a wave moving out from her, he could see the children fidgeting, starting to cry. Stupid woman!

There was enough room between children sitting against the hallway walls to push his way through. He got to the screamer and peeled her hands away from her face. He got into her face and hissed, "Shut up."

Her fingers pulled at his hand and she mewled.

He got his mouth right to her ear. "Don't make me slap you in front of these children. And I *will* slap you." He was incensed, and it showed in his voice. Here were a bunch of seven-year-olds acting like grownups, and a grownup acting like an infant.

His threat shut her up. Her eyes met his and he gave her his best gang-control glare. She cowered from him, but she also shut up.

He stood up, panting, trying to beat back the anger and get it out of his voice. "Everything's okay, everybody," he said. He turned to smile at the nearby children. "She's all better now and everyone is fine."

"Dad!" He heard Holly's voice and looked around. She was standing, farther down the hall, and trying to come for him.

He tiptoed through the children's legs and met her halfway, pulling her up into his arms. "Everything's okay, baby. Let's sit down."

He expected to hear the train sound of a tornado, the crunching of breaking wood, something, by now. But there was nothing but the murmurs of children, a few of them still crying, the shushing of teachers trying to calm their charges.

"Are we going home?" said Holly.

"Soon," he said. "Or to Aunt Sherryl's maybe, or to daycare." A couple children had wiggled their way to the side enough to allow him to sit down. He thanked them, sat, and gathered Holly into his lap.

"After-school care," she said, irritated. "I'm too old for daycare."

"Yes, you are."

"You smell funny."

Fear. He suspected that he smelled like fear, the chemical stink of sweat from a man who was afraid for these children's lives. He held her tighter, closed his eyes, and waited for the thing to come upon them.

* * *

The sound of her own name brought Malika out of the total darkness of unconsciousness.

She was wet. And she hurt. Her head hurt, and her shoulders hurt. For a few seconds, that's all she knew.

Then she heard her name again. She opened her eyes, only then understanding they had been closed. She could see some light, but in crazy geometric patterns, like some 20th century art form—she tried to remember from Art Appreciation last year which movement that might be. Op maybe? Or Cubism?

She was on her stomach and tried to turn over, to get a better look at her surroundings, but she couldn't move.

"Malika!"

Maybe I'm dead. Maybe that's God, and I'm dead, and I'm being called. Or Jesus, I suppose. Or—

"Malika, for God's sake!"

Would God use his own name in vain? Could it even *be* in vain if it were God Himself using it? That was a puzzler. One to ask her pastor.

"Are you alive?"

Wouldn't God know the answer to that? Then her mind swam a bit clearer, and she understood it was someone here, on the planet Earth, calling to her.

"Adam?" she said, but her voice came out a croak. She tried it louder. "Adam, is that you?"

"Meek!" he shouted, and then he started crying. Last time he had done that—or last time she had heard it—was the day she told him it was over between them.

"Don't cry," she said, but too softly for him to hear. Where the hell was she? In school, she supposed, but where? She tried to remember the day until now. She remembered lunch, clearly, with Dylan. Then nothing much in her memory from the afternoon, but she knew it had to be afternoon. No, she did remember, being in chorus, her last class. *I'm probably late to debate.* Mr. Evans was going to be mad at her. Dylan would be even madder, and Sarah and Cody would get a win by default. It didn't count toward a grade, but it counted toward her pride. She tried to get up. She had to get there before she forfeited.

But when she tried to push herself up, nothing happened. She felt a tile floor beneath her palms, and a puddle of water on the tile, and the weight of something across her shoulders. She felt her butt—nothing on top of it—and her legs.

No. Wrong. She couldn't feel her legs. She tried moving them, tried kicking out.

Nothing. She was sending signals to her legs, ordering them to move, but nothing was happening.

She began to panic. "Hey, help! I can't move!"

"I'm here." Adam. He had control of himself again.

"What's wrong? I can't move."

"Tornado. A tornado hit the school."

That didn't make any sense. Tornado was wind and maybe rain and—Oh. Like it had blown the roof off and it had come down on her. Something like that?

"Is the roof on top of me?"

"I guess, maybe. I'm going to go look. I'll be back in two minutes, tops."

Don't go. She bit her lips closed to keep from screaming the words. In the meantime, she tried to move what she could, inventorying her body. Her butt was free. Her forearms were free. Her chest was pinned to the floor. Her legs—she didn't know, couldn't feel them at all. *What if I'm paralyzed?*

The thought made her struggle to free her arms. Maybe she could pull herself out with her arms somehow. The right arm seemed to have more freedom of motion. She yanked, and pressed, and wiggled it back and forth, trying to shift something so she could get it free. Even if she could just reach back and feel her neck, make sure her spine wasn't broken. She pushed down onto the wet tile with all her might with her left forearm, trying to lever herself up far enough to free her right arm.

A crunching sound stopped her. She had shifted something over her body, but suddenly—belatedly—realized maybe she shouldn't. What if her struggles brought something else down on her?

Or pinned her hands tightly too? She didn't think she could stand that, being pinned from fingertip to toes. She eased back down and realized her ear was resting in the puddle. At least the water seemed to be getting shallower, not deeper.

"It's draining away somewhere," she said to herself, and being able to think that through logically made her feel better. Good, on the draining. At least she wouldn't drown in a puddle while she was pinned here.

"Meek?" It was Adam again.

"I'm here. Alive, but stuck tight."

"It's a bus."

That made no sense. Maybe her head was damaged worse than she knew. "*What's* a bus?"

"A school bus, one of the small ones, slammed into the wall of the building outside. The wall came down, and some of the roof too."

"Is the bus on top of me?"

"No, but it came a couple feet through the wall."

"Like in driver's ed." One of their classmates had famously put a driver's ed car into a brick retaining wall last year.

"Geez, Meek, I hadn't thought of that in a year. But yeah, like that."

"By the Hand of God, though, not a student driver."

"Something like that. I'm going to go get you help."

"No! Don't leave me here."

"I can't get you out on my own. There's—" She could almost hear him thinking through a nice way to say something unpleasant. That was Adam for you. "A lot of stuff piled up. And it's like a maze, like that kid's game, you know, pick-up sticks?"

"Sure," she said. "I remember it."

"I don't want to touch the wrong stick. So I have to get someone—or a few people."

"Please. Don't go." Had he said that to her earlier today? And she had turned and gone, hadn't she? "Stay and talk to me."

"But—"

"They'll be coming. Adam, it's a school. There's been a tornado? Fire, police, they'll be here, walk around the whole school, see the problem."

"Well...," he said, hesitating.

"They'll have equipment, right? You and even a dozen other kids won't be able to get me out any faster than one fireman with the right equipment."

"I can't do *nothing*."

"Talk to me. That's a lot more than nothing, I swear."

"Aww, Meek." He sighed, a shaky sound. "Are you hurt?"

"I'm talking to you, right? So not awful bad."

"Can you move?"

"No. Not a lot."

"Are you bleeding?"

God, she hadn't even thought. "Not that I know of. It's kind of dark in here." What if the puddle beneath her was partly her own blood? Or all her own blood? The idea made her dizzy. She pushed that aside and clamped onto consciousness, holding to it like a life raft.

"At least you're talking. Making sense, even."

Was she? Good. "Thank you for staying."

"Look, every few minutes, I'm going to run outside and call for help, okay? I can't just do nothing at all. Couldn't stand to. I'll run right back here, I swear."

"Okay," she said. "That's okay. Just...don't leave me. Please."

"I'm right here," he said. "I'm staying right here until they get you out."

* * *

Sherryl struggled out from under Jim. The wind was howling now and she heard, at a distance, the sound of something hitting the roof or wall of the care center. The thing was nearly upon her. She shoved the wheelchair away and crawled out, leaving Jim half under the bed.

Best place for him.

She grabbed the blanket and tossed it over Jim, then tried to wrestle the mattress off the bed. She'd fall down with it over the both of them and hope for the best.

The noise of the wind grew louder, and when she thought it couldn't get any worse, louder still, a shriek of a noise. The mattress was stuck or—maybe it was locked down somehow.

She glanced down at Jim, saw he was fully covered, even his head. He was batting ineffectually at the blankets.

And the next thing she knew, she was getting hurled through the air.

Flying. Like Peter Pan, she thought.

And then, as the glass from the window exploded without a sound, her back slammed against the far wall.

The shriek of the wind was deafening. She realized the glass must have crashed noisily when it exploded, but it couldn't be heard because of the wind. She pulled her T-shirt over her face, hoping to minimize any damage from the swirling glass, and closed her eyes. She heard a wrenching sound, and could see light through her T-shirt.

She risked a peek upward with one eye, and she saw the roof had come off. As she watched, the outer wall collapsed inward.

She felt herself lifting from the floor, the tornado—for that's surely what this was—trying to pull her out of the room, and she grappled blindly behind herself, trying to find purchase. Her hand caught the edge of the closet door, a thin metal folding one. The force of the wind was pulling her across the carpet now, the friction shoving her pants legs up, and then her shirt. The closet door lurched out of its tracks and she slid three feet in a split second, the door coming with her. Then the left side wall to the room fell outward, and then the one to her right, at the head of the bed, fell inward like a second domino.

She was screaming by then, screaming so hard her throat felt raw, but she couldn't hear herself over the wind.

And then her body quit sliding. The wind died. She clamped her mouth shut and let go of the door, which moaned as it settled back, one connection to the track still in place. She glanced back. It had twisted itself into a modern sculpture.

She was alive. The wall back here, the one against the hallway, hadn't fallen. The side walls had come mostly down, leaning toward the east side of the building. There was drywall and a long thin board across her feet.

She kicked them away and inventoried her body. Back still hurt. Carpet burns just above her waist. She patted her face quickly and looked at her hands. No blood.

But there were nail-studded boards and broken glass all around her. If she wasn't careful in what she did next, she would be bleeding.

Jim.

The wall had fallen onto the bed. And onto the floor on both sides of it.

I should have gotten him farther underneath the bed.

The bed was still there, miraculously, pulled out from the wall, but still pointed the same direction. It must be really heavy to have withstood the tug of the wind.

Shedding bits of glass, she stood. She let her head fall forward and shook it, trying to get all the glass shards out of her hair. Then she brushed her hair with cold fingertips, brushed off her shoulders.

She could hear screams and shouts behind her.

It was easier to back up into the hall than to go forward,

toward Jim, where she wanted to go. Okay, so she'd go out and find someone to help her get Jim out from under the fallen wall. She picked her way to the door and looked out into the hallway.

The entire wing of the nursing home was a scene out of a nightmare. The central hallway stood, but the roof over it was gone. Cloud-filtered sunlight illuminated a hallway filled with debris. It looked like a sloppy construction sight. Voices came from the other side of the hall, from frightened patients, calling out, and she could hear a man weeping piteously. She could see into one door over there. The walls hadn't seemed to have fallen in the rooms on that side of the hall. So they were probably better off on that side. Maybe roof bits had fallen on them, but from the sound of many voices, most of them had survived. They were just scared.

Who could blame them?

There were twenty rooms on this side, gutted as far as she could see, like Jim's, and probably more damage on the other wing of the building. The central area with all the windows and the cafeteria had probably taken a lot of damage.

Some nurses and orderlies were going to be hurt too. She couldn't see any. The chance of her getting any help in the next few minutes? Miniscule.

It was up to her to find Jim and get him out from under the fallen wall.

* * *

After five minutes had passed, Greg began to hope that they were safe. After ten minutes, he knew they were. He put down Holly and apologized to the screamer he'd threatened on his way past her—not that the apology would stop her complaining to everyone she knew and probably to the chief, but whatever—and apologized again to the teacher with the special needs kid, who seemed fine now, chattering with a neighbor like nothing had ever been wrong.

At the bottom of the staircase, he clapped for silence and told everyone to stay put until he or the other policeman told them it was safe. Then Greg jogged up the steps into the hallway, stopping at the fire door to listen before opening it. The hall was peaceful. He slipped into the first room and looked out the windows. No hail, very light rain, and a much brighter sky.

He thumbed on his radio and got Massey. "Yeah, I'm here," he said, "in the cafeteria. Where are you?"

"Upstairs. I think it's passed us by. Meet me at the front door."

"Roger that."

They met there and went outside, stopping under the overhang out of the light rain. Both looked to the southwest across the street. Nothing there. No tornado, no black debris cloud. In fact, it looked lighter in that direction, as if the storm was clearing. Any hail that had fallen had already melted.

Massey radioed in to the dispatcher. He got nothing but static. "I'll try the car radio." He trotted off toward it.

The streets looked normal, except for extra paper trash tumbling along the curbs. A stream of water moved slowly toward the drains. All the abandoned cars of parents were lined up, some of their doors still open, looking like something out of a Hollywood zombie film. But then a car passed on the road, swerving around the cars still lined up in the street, and then a second car came along. Behind him, the door opened and a chunky young woman came out.

He turned. "You a teacher?"

"A mom. Is it safe now?"

"Looks like it missed us. Would you go down to the cafeteria and make the announcement that it's all clear? I'll do it on the other side." He realized all the parents from the cars must have gone down the other side of the basement with Massey and the principal—he'd only had children and teachers on his side.

Massey had shut off lights and siren. He got out of the patrol car and trotted up, calling, "It's gone."

"The tornado?"

He came up, wild-eyed. "The station. The police station is gone."

Captain T

We're coming up about a mile, I think, behind the tornado, which is still impossible to see. It's a real rainy sucker, this one, so we're showing you the debris field instead as we literally chase it, from behind, taking care not to overtake it. All the roads here are north-south or east-west, so we're having to turn up and down streets to follow its path. So right now we're coming up on the high school, according to our GPS.

Here's a couple of kids now. Let me roll down my window. "Guys. Did the tornado hit you? Hit the school?"

"Took out our stadium and the parking lot. My car is like totally wrecked. Piled on another car. My dad is going to kill me."

"Any students hurt?"

"I don't know."

Well, viewers, we'll drive on up and see what has happened. Rest assured, we'll stay out of the way of the rescuers, and lend a hand the moment they ask us to. Okay, here, on this street about six houses look pretty much destroyed. Felix is filming his side of the street, but it's just as bad on my side. I hope they had cellars, or were someplace else this afternoon. We need to turn right again here to keep to the debris field.

Yeah, look at this, viewers—can you tell this is a wider path here than it was right at the edge of town? The way these houses are mowed down, the width here, I'm guessing it was an EF3 or 4 when it hit. There's the school parking lot, over there. Wow, we're going to need to get off this street—too much debris in the middle of it. I think we'll park, Felix, and walk through the hammered town of Fidelity, following the twister's path for now, interviewing anyone who feels like talking.

Catch you later, loyal viewers.

Chapter 6

Greg said, "The station is gone? You mean they're dead?"

"No, the dispatcher says they made it down to the EOC." That was underground. "But the building is totaled, and the stairs are blocked. They're fine, but they can't get out yet."

"What else is hit?"

"Not all known yet. Downtown, though. Just like that guy told you would happen. Went almost exactly through the crossroads of the two highways. It'll be stores, city hall, the courthouse."

"Holy shit," he breathed. He shook off his shock. "We have to get over there."

"Yeah."

"I guess the chief was smart to put us out on patrol." He thought of what it'd be like if all the town's police force were stuck inside the basement right now.

"I wonder how many were out like us," Massey said.

"However many, we're it now. You, me, whoever else. Is the fire department okay?" The fire station was newer, and on the west side of town, out of the probable path of the tornado.

"I didn't ask, but they didn't mention, so let's assume so. They're going to have to effect the rescue of the people in the

EOC."

"We gotta figure this out." He had to find something to do with Holly. He couldn't take her along on patrol.

Massey must have read his mind. "They'll have to keep the kids right here. Parents will have been—" his mouth twisted as the thought hit him "—hurt, some of them. Others, the ones with cars here, are going to go home and find their houses gone. Maybe they'll come back here, for lack of anywhere else to shelter."

"I imagine they'd want to look through the damage at home, try to save a few things."

"With a little kid in tow? I hope they think smarter than that. Anyway, it'll take some time to sort out. So you can leave her here, I think."

"I'll talk to the principal, make sure she gets something organized, has someone to supervise the kids—maybe until nightfall." Maybe all night. The school might end up a community shelter.

Massey said, "At least they have food in the cafeteria. They can serve dinner there if they need to. Breakfast, even."

"Yeah. You get back on the radio and try and contact Fire, talk to Chief Stephens, have them decide where to use us best, all that. I'll find the principal and get this shelter thing started."

He turned and went indoors, through a stream of children and adults. They seemed to be hesitating at the door before going outside. Greg raised his hands for quiet, and he got it surprisingly fast. "The storm has passed, so you can go outside to your cars. There's been some damage in town, though. Be careful driving. There is going be stuff on some roads, and you don't want to get a flat tire. If you need to, moms and dads, you can come back here, or bring your children back for a short time if you can't find your regular sitter. Who's a teacher here?"

A young man with John Lennon glasses came forward. Greg lowered his voice to speak to him. "We're going to have to organize this. There are houses down, stores down, all over town.

Not all these kids will have a home to go to. If any child doesn't have an adult show up, let's keep them here for now, where we know they're safe."

"What if they walk home every day because they live right by here?"

Greg hesitated. "Let me think it through. I suppose if it's within two or three blocks, they'll be safe. The storm struck six blocks south, it sounds like. What would happen if they didn't follow their routine and walk home?"

"We'd have parents or babysitters calling and showing up. Well, I guess if they've heard about the tornado, they'll start showing up any second now anyway, panicked."

"Okay, then keep the kids all here. Let children leave only with parents or known guardians. Get the security guard at the door and don't let any unaccompanied kid wander out, okay? Check ID of adults coming in. Will you organize that with the guard?"

"Sure."

Greg caught sight of the principal, surrounded by a gaggle of adults. "Do that, and thanks," he said to the teacher. He walked over toward the principal and held his hand up until she looked his way. "I need to talk with you. In two minutes," he called, holding up two fingers.

She nodded and turned to answer a question.

Greg walked back to his staircase, where a few teachers stood along with the receptionist, obediently waiting for his okay. "Everyone can come upstairs now," he said.

The receptionist turned to go back down, and he leaned forward to touch her shoulder. "I think the principal probably needs you."

"Right. Thanks," she said, and hustled off toward the offices.

"Do the cell phones work?" one of the teachers asked.

"No idea. Possibly some towers are down," he said. "Give it a try."

He waited at the end of the hall nearest the central area and blocked people from swarming the front door. When they seemed to all be in the hall, chattering excitedly, he dug out his whistle and blew it. It took twice, and finally they shut up.

"Okay, here's the new rules," he said. "If your mom or dad comes to pick you up, you can go home. Everybody else stays after school until they do."

A babble of voices broke out. The teacher closest to him made herself heard. "What about us?"

"Check with the principal on that." If he were in charge, he'd make sure all the teachers stayed to supervise—but then, some of them might have children themselves, in the middle school or high school, and like any parent, they'd want to check on them. He looked at the swarming mass of people and raised his voice. "Everybody go back to your classrooms, okay? Just for a minute. Your parents will come and get you when they arrive."

"I take the bus," piped up one boy.

"We'll find out if it's coming," Greg said, feeling well out of his depth. He saw Holly squirming her way forward between the other students. "Just go to your classrooms, and be patient. Maybe you can draw, or play a game, or sing," he said. Definitely out of his depth on that.

The same teachers who had gotten the exodus organized most quickly were also those who herded their charges back into their rooms first. The screamer even seemed to be able to function now that the danger was past.

Holly came up to him and he squatted in front of her. "Can I go home with you?" she said.

"No, sweetie. I have to work. You can stay here for a little bit. If it gets to be supper time and I'm not here, they'll get you something to eat."

"Can I go to Aunt Sherryl's?"

"Maybe. I'll try and get her on the phone. If she comes, or Malika, you can go with them, okay? Or Mrs. Maberry from next door, or a police officer in uniform. But no one else."

"Stranger danger," she said.

Strangers probably were not going be the worst threat today. But he said, "That's right, sweetie. I wish I didn't have to work, but I do."

"You help people."

"Yes, I have to try and help," he said. "Now get into your classroom before I get you in trouble for being late."

"I have a new joke."

"Great," he said.

"What's yellow and goes *mmmmmmmmmmmmmm*?"

"I don't know."

"An electric lemon!" She laughed, then turned before he could stop her and skipped down the hall.

He almost chased her for a hug and kiss, but he couldn't. He had to get back to the principal and make sure she was on top of her new duties, then get going with Massey to do whatever they could in the destruction zone.

As he walked toward the office, he thought of all that might need to get done. Rescue. Directing traffic. Taking people to the hospital. Ideally, Fire would do the heavy rescue. Ambulances would get the injured treated or transported. And there were more important things to do than direct traffic. He wondered if there'd be looting, especially at the downtown stores. Probably. He wished for a cadre of private security guards to station on every block, a uniformed presence to deter looters, even if they didn't have the power to arrest anyone.

But it was going to be all up to them—however many of the force there were left on the streets—to do it all.

When he got back to the car, Massey said, "We had four cars out on patrol, but one isn't answering."

"Who?"

"Magarelli and Simms."

A rookie and the only other woman on the force except for the chief. "Geez. I hope they're okay."

"I told everyone we're headed back to the station, if we can get to it. I told them to meet us north of there on Elm, the first place the street is clear."

"Good idea."

They were silent as they drove south. It was only a half-mile to the main east-west road through town, called Main Street while it went through Fidelity, and an alternate US highway outside of town. The debris on the streets swirled in a light wind as they drove through it. Greg could tell when they were nearing the path of the twister's destruction—there was far more debris flung out in every direction with every block they drove.

Perversely, the sun came out from behind a cloud to illuminate the scene of devastation ahead. A swath that looked to be a block wide was a brown and gray streak where once there had been homes and stores.

"It's like someone took a steam iron to it, and flattened it," said Massey.

Greg had been imagining something similar, a giant dragging a smoldering log. They pulled up to the edge of it and both got out of the car, leaving the doors open. People were stumbling around in the debris, calling names. Blood was visible on more than one of them, and a few were plastered with dirt. He recognized a few faces, but other faces were so covered with mud or blood that he couldn't have recognized his own mother had she been one of them.

"We should get to our meeting," said Greg.

Massey said, "I feel like we should help them."

So did Greg, but he knew the emergency protocols. "We are. We will. Just let's break out assignments between the six guys on duty now and then we'll do all we can, as fast as we can."

Back in the car, Massey drove over two blocks until they were at Elm. They drove forward again into the debris field. This one was a bit farther north, showing how the path of the tornado had gone east-northeast. It seemed to have hit the crossroads dead-on.

But west of there, it had hit the south part of town. On the east side, it'd be the north part of town.

For the first time, Greg realized that meant his house may have been hit.

But running there right now wouldn't change anything. If it was gone, it was gone. He had work to do for other people first.

Massey stopped in the street at the edge of the debris field. Before he exited the car, Greg tried phoning his aunt—no service. He tried Malika's house. No service. He assumed the cell phones were out everywhere. He typed in "we're fine" as a text to his aunt and pressed send, hoping it would go through soon. He hoped he'd get one back that said the same thing.

The first prowl car came in behind them two minutes later, carrying Evans and Brinkley, and the four men began to talk.

Massey said, "Maybe one of us should stay with his car at all times, and coordinate everything on the radio."

One of the newcomers, Evans, said, "We still have Dispatch, even if they're trapped underground. Radios are still working, so we can leave messages there. The chief says the fire department will get them out, and we're to help citizens. That way, all six of us can be on the ground."

"Right," said Greg. "I think we need to divide town into thirds. Everything west of here. Everything from Elm to, say, Magnolia. Everything east of Magnolia."

"Sounds right," said Evans. "Do we know where Magarelli and Simms were?"

"Can get that from Dispatch," said Massey.

Brinkley had been silent until now. Greg turned to him. "You okay?"

"I think my house might be in the path."

"You won't be able to work if you're worrying about your family."

"No. No one was home. My wife works way down south. She'll freak when she hears about this, but she was well out of it, from what we hear. It's just the house. We just had it re-sided."

They all nodded, sympathizing. Evans said, "It's okay, man, the insurance will cover it."

Greg said, "Okay, so when the last car gets here, we'll divide up the town, and whoever's section of town it is, keep an eye out for the missing patrol team." And he slapped Brinkley's arm. "I hope your house is okay."

"I'll find out eventually," he said, faintly.

Greg looked around. "Where are the other two guys?"

Massey went to radio them and came back to report on what he'd found. The last car couldn't get through to the north of town. The tornado had effectively split the town in two, and it'd take some heavy equipment to clear any road. Quickly, they re-divided the town. Massey and Greg would do everything east of Central, where the elementary school was, and Evans and Brinkley would do everything west of there, cutting southwest to stay close to the tornado track. The guys stuck on the south side of town could work the whole town from that side, entering the tornado damage area from the south.

As they drove back to Central, Greg radioed Dispatch and found out where the missing patrol team had been at last contact—northwest of town, on the country roads, just as he and Massey had been southwest. "They should be out of the disaster zone, then," said Greg. "So why can't anyone raise them?"

Dispatch said, "Working on it."

"What's the news on the fire department? Is their station standing?"

"Yeah, the tornado hit north of it by about five blocks. They're doing a windshield survey right now with two trucks. And they have someone trying to get them through to the north side way out on the edge of town, on County A, and they'll check from that side too. We'll coordinate all that."

"Great. So what do we do first?"

"Hold on for the chief."

Rosemary Stephens's voice came on the radio. "What sort of equipment do you have?"

Greg told her what he knew was in the trunk.

"Gloves?"

Greg looked at Massey, who shook his head. "We'll try and find some," said Greg.

"Do that. Try to get into downtown at Central and help who you can. Keep an eye out for looters. Find any, and cuff 'em, bring 'em back to the car, and shove them in the back. Forget about them while you go back to help. Any heavy lifting, leave for Fire. Radio in for medical care. There's a triage center at the fire station."

Massey muttered, "Which no one can get through to from here."

Chief Stephens went on, "Send the ones who can get there to triage. We'll get ambulances up from Cinci or down from the north too."

"Copy that," said Greg. "We're pulling onto Central now. Anything else?"

"Keep people from driving into the debris. We need barricades up."

Massey and Greg exchanged a look. Barricades weren't something they had. A dozen flares was about the most they could provide.

"We'll get road crews on that from the county, right away, but do what you can until then. And report in any fires, gas leaks— like that. And when the fire department reports in, you may get reassigned. So be ready to move quickly."

"Right," said Greg. "We're going on our handhelds now. Over and out."

Captain T

The tornado that slammed through this small heartland town has, according to the radar, likely roped out, so we're staying here for a little while, interviewing victims.

We've walked all the way in to the middle of town, where there once was a brick courthouse, a police station, and a few dozen thriving local businesses. Now, as you can see, there are tumbled bricks, and glass, and the walking wounded. From the sorts of damage I'm seeing, I'm guessing this one will end up being called a high EF3 or low EF4.

We've found this tree—pan up, Felix—that's still standing at the edge of the worst damage, and you see that? That's a refrigerator door up there. And I found this bicycle which I know you won't believe is a bike, but get a close-up. See? Here's the spokes, and the seat stem. I hope no one was on it when this happened.

We have a car here, on its side, and look at this rebar that punched right through the metal roof. Up ahead, beyond the barricades, the firemen working noisily there with generators and winches—they're trying to unbury the police station. We think that no one is hurt inside, at least, and because they made it to a well built basement, they should be fine. There are plenty of policemen out on the streets—we've seen two ourselves in the last few minutes. They don't want us to bother them, understandably, but I'd like to ask when they're getting to the rest of these buildings, and in what order. There must be other survivors buried in these stores and office buildings.

And, I'm afraid, there are likely to be more than a few bodies buried here too. Rain-wrapped tornados are dangerous. If you don't hear a siren, don't see the TV, don't hear the warning on the radio—or don't heed the warning—you can't see it coming. There's rain, and then suddenly, poof, you're gone.

On that somber note, I'll close out this video post. Stay safe, people. Look at this shot of a devastated downtown, and, as you do, please remember to obey all storm warnings.

Chapter 7

"I don't like it," said Massey.

"What?"

"That we talked about where we were going on the radio with the car down south. I wish we'd been able to do it face to face."

"You're thinking...?"

"Looters. We just told them where we won't be."

Greg looked ahead, to the damage area, to the mud-splattered people digging through the ruins of their lives. "I can't imagine anyone would loot at a time like this."

Massey snorted. "Failure of imagination on your part."

"We can only do what we can do. Let's go see what."

As they walked forward, they passed the first damaged house. A rear porch had been ripped off, and a gutter. An older woman was outside, looking up at her gutters.

"You okay, ma'am? Anyone hurt?" Greg called over.

"Better than most," she called back.

The opposite side of the street was a pay parking lot, half empty. At the far side, cars had been pushed into one another. One alarm still screeched.

"I'm going to run over and shut that off," said Massey.

Greg continued down the street. More and more debris filled

the sidewalk and street. The next house from the old woman's had taken more damage. Shingles off the roof, collapsed chimney, cracked windows. Picking his way through the debris, Greg made his way to the front door, which he saw was popped open an inch. He knocked on it, calling, "Anyone home?"

No one answered. After twenty seconds, he knocked again and pushed at the door. It was stuck fast. At least it'd take a thief some effort to get into. He hoped no one was in there, hurt. But he hadn't the equipment to force the door and had to move on.

His shoes crunched over broken glass. If he was going to pick around in any of this, he really did need some work gloves. They had latex gloves, he knew, but nothing heavier. Well, hell. He made his way back to the house with the gutter damage and went up to the woman. "Ma'am?"

"Yes?"

He introduced himself. "We're going to need work gloves. Do you have anything like that you could donate—work or garden gloves, something like that?"

"I have some garden gloves."

"Anything will help."

"Let me pull them out of my garage, and I'll catch up to you when I find them."

Next house wasn't really a house at all—not any more. The nearest wall still stood, and the center of the house had a maze of pipes intact. But everything else that had been someone's home was now collapsed into the center or blowing in the breeze around them. He saw a doll on the ground and hoped its owner had been at the elementary school and not here when the winds had destroyed this home.

Papers were blowing about—could be important papers, insurance or car titles, or junk mail. He stepped over a dented toaster oven and into a patch of clothes, still on hangers. One dress was inside a plastic hanging bag. His ex had kept her wedding gown like that until the marriage had started to go bad.

Then she got rid of it.

Greg had an urge to pick up the dress, the papers, to save these important things for people. But he had to let it go. There were living people who needed help, and mere things had to be ignored for now. Ahead of him was the center of the destruction. Not a single tree was still standing. Old oaks, maples, and flowering fruit trees laden with spring blossoms had lined these streets just an hour ago. Now there was one, a black walnut, he thought, that looked like a fat broken toothpick, sticking up maybe ten feet, the upper part gone. The remainder was split down the middle and totally denuded of bark. A few of the trees were still here, in the yards, but uprooted and stripped of everything green, with clothes and draperies and shingles draped over their bare branches like tinsel.

Ahead in the street, next to a dirty ball of a tree's roots, a woman had waylaid Massey. Either he had gotten the car alarm off or it had gone off on its own, and now the woman was tugging at Massey's sleeve, talking earnestly to him. Massey looked up and waved him over.

Greg got there as fast as the debris underfoot would let him. "What's up?" he called as he approached.

"This woman has lost a child," said Massey.

Greg moved to her side.

"Now try and calm down, ma'am, and describe him," Massey was saying.

Now that he was there, Greg could see that the woman was crying and her hand was shaking where it gripped Massey's uniform shirt. "He's black," she said.

Massey's eyebrow moved a fraction. The woman was middle-aged and white, and except for the mud streaking her face, pale. Younger people were more likely to be in mixed-race couples, but for her generation, in Fidelity, it was fairly unusual.

"And he's got curly hair. He's about twelve pounds."

Greg's mind took a second to make the jump, adding up her

age and the description. "Ma'am, are you talking about a dog?"

"My baby!" she wailed.

Greg was glad her face was turned to him now so she couldn't see Massey's look of disgust. "We'll keep an eye out. What's your dog's name?"

"Tinker. For Tinkerbell, but I never called him by his whole name."

"Thanks for telling us. Now, is anyone else in your house hurt?"

"It was just me at home."

"Which one is yours?"

She pointed with a shaky hand to the house with the pipes and one wall. "I was in the bathroom, but he was on his doggie bed. Out in the living room."

There was no living room any more. Greg doubted the dog had survived, and it was a wonder the woman had. "But you're okay? No cuts, broken bones?"

"I'm fine."

"We'll do what we can. Is there anywhere you can go now—to a friend's or relative's?"

"I can't leave until I find Tinker!"

"Sure, sure," said Greg.

Massey had schooled his expression again and said, "Best of luck to you. We have to look for survivors."

They continued into the heart of the tornado zone. Beyond the woman's house, the totality of the destruction made it impossible to tell how many homes there had been. Only his knowledge of the size of a lot in town helped him pick out one property from the next.

"Damn," said Massey, stumbling over something.

"Be careful." If there were only six police officers available in a town of 42,000, they couldn't afford to have one down with injuries.

"I'm fine." Massey looked around and lowered his voice. "Do

you think anyone in these houses survived?"

Greg shook his head. "I don't see how."

"What the hell can we do here, then?"

Greg shook his head again, more slowly. "Let's get close to where the basements might have been, call out, see if we hear anyone calling back for help. If we don't hear anything, we move on to the next street." Ahead of them, for about half a block, everything had been flattened and blown up, or blown out. Then just blown around. A file folder detached itself from the mess ahead, opened up, and papers skittered out. "Is the wind picking up again?" he said.

"Maybe. Feels like it might be."

Greg looked down the line of destruction toward the west. Because all the buildings had been mowed down, he could see a long way. A high, vast cloud was coming this way. It had flattened out high up, but over that, a puff stuck out over it, like a mushroom cloud, white in the sun. At the bottom of the cloud, everything was black. "We're going to get more rain. Look." He pointed.

Massey breathed, "Shit. That's not going to help at all."

"It's still a few miles off. There was a line of squalls on TV. Could be that we'll get a lot more, storm after storm." He checked his watch. "I think we should call in and get a weather report."

"Let's finish here."

They called out to anyone who might need their help. Then they were quiet for thirty seconds after each round of shouting. Not a sound came back. There was a siren in the distance, but nothing else.

"Back to the car. Next street, I guess," said Greg. He felt utterly useless in the face of all this destruction. When they passed the dog woman, Greg called to her, "Ma'am? I'm sorry, what's your name?"

"Rowena Baker." There was a Baker on the city council— maybe she was related.

"It's going to rain again, Ms. Baker. It'd be best if you got under cover." And were sitting down someplace when the dimension of her loss hit her—not just the dog, but her whole house and everything inside—in case she went into shock. "Sure we can't drop you someplace?"

"I have to find Tinker," she said.

Greg gave it up and they went back to the car to radio in for a weather update. On the way, the woman with the gutters hailed him and brought him a pair of pink gardening gloves, small-looking, but better than nothing.

"Love the color," said Massey, when she had left. "You can have those."

"I like the color more than the red of my blood." They climbed in the car, and Greg got on the radio while Massey fired up the engine.

"We're still under the tornado watch," said the dispatcher. "But no news of another tornado sighting. We're going to send you addresses from the 911 calls we're getting in your section of town. The chief is prioritizing them, and you'll get the top ones only. Chief says, use your judgment on them from there, unless you get an order from her or a call from the fire chief."

"Is there any chance of power coming back? If people start to drive around, trying to get to family, we won't have traffic lights. And it's going to be dark sooner than we want." He imagined dozens of fender benders complicating his job.

"They're on it."

"You'll tell us if there's any more weather alerts, right?"

"Roger that."

"We're moving on to Hickory." He signed off and said to Massey, "I don't envy the power workers up on poles in a storm."

"I don't envy us out in a storm."

"Or the people, digging through the scraps of their homes, out in the storm, as night falls." His mind turned again to Holly. It was hard to keep it from doing so, even though he had seen with his own eyes that she was safe. He asked Massey, "Have you called your wife?"

"She works in Springfield. I'm sure she's fine."

"But she doesn't know you're safe. The news will have this by now. She'll hear about it, and she'll be worried."

"Right. Good point." He stopped the car, lights still flashing but siren silent, and dug out his phone. "I'm getting no service."

Greg checked his again. Also nothing. "Text her."

"I'll do it later when I get some bars."

Greg though about offering to do it for him, but kept his mouth shut. No reason to nag and antagonize the man he had to work with. "Do you think we should split up, each take a different street?"

"No. I want you to watch my back. And what if we have to pick up something heavy to get it off a victim?"

"True." Greg stifled a sigh as they turned up the first clear east-west street, then turned right again, back toward the damage zone. "I still don't know what we're doing to help. What we *can* do." Getting up close to those destroyed houses had shaken him, made him feel too small and useless in the face of such a power.

"I don't know either until we do it."

The next block had similar damage to Central. They found an older man and a woman sitting on the curb, among the wreckage of their home. The man's shirt was off, and he was pressing it against the woman's head. The shirt was red with her blood, soaked nearly through. She was leaning heavily on the man.

Massey muttered, "I'll get the first aid kit and radio in the injury. It looks serious."

Greg bent down. "Hey. I'm Officer Duncan. What can I do to help?"

"Can you call an ambulance?" said the man.

"Already done." The woman's eyes were closed. "Is she conscious?"

"In and out," said the man.

"Which house is yours?"

"That one." He pointed.

Greg looked. It was utterly destroyed. Not even pipes sticking out of the ground on this one. "How'd you make it?"

"Basement, but stuff fell on us, boards and whatnot. The stove came down, but thank God it missed us. Some glass got Millie."

Greg wondered how the man had gotten them both out after that. "Are you hurt at all?"

He shook his head. "Nothing that can't wait. You know, it doesn't sound like a train at all."

"The tornado, you mean?"

"It's wind. It sounds like wind, but so *much* wind. It's hard to describe."

The woman moaned, just as Massey came up with a first aid kit, already gloved and ready to treat her. "Let's look at that a second," he said.

Greg backed off a step and watched, ready to lend a hand if asked. The man took the shirt away and fresh blood welled along a cut that stretched from the woman's hairline back through her hair. Hard to see very well, except for the blood draining out.

"God," said the man. "Will she make it?"

"Head wounds bleed a lot more than cuts other places," said Greg, trying to reassure the man—and the injured woman, if she could hear him.

"How much blood can a person lose?" The man held up the bloody shirt.

Massey was cutting away her hair, trying to get a better look at the injury. "If we shave this, I think we can butterfly it. It's not terribly deep," he said. "Duncan, look for a razor in the kit."

Greg pawed through the kit, which was too damned small in the face of all the injuries they were likely to find. No razor or even razor blade.

Greg looked around himself. Probably twenty or thirty plastic razors scattered around the ground out here. Somewhere, under all the mess.

Massey made do with the scissors, snipping her hair short. He had Greg take a two-by-two and pat away the blood as he butterflied the length of the cut. In five minutes, the woman's wound was barely bleeding. Massey did good first-aid work.

Greg looked up. The leading edge of the next storm was drifting overhead. No rain yet, but Greg thought there would be soon.

Massey applied the last butterfly strip and tore open a gauze patch. "Hold this on," he told the man. "And I'll leave you a second bandage, in case that one is soaked. And tell me about your neighbors up and down the block. Would any of them been home?"

The man could be seen trying to shift his attention from his wife. "Not the Macklebees. They both work." He glanced across the street. "There's a young mother over there, in that—well, what used to be that house there. With a baby and a toddler. I don't know their names yet. I'm not sure if they were home or not. She drove a green sedan, but I don't see it, so maybe she was out somewhere."

There were three cars visible. One was flipped on its roof and one was on its side, the undercarriage pointed their way. Greg would check it in a second. "The Honda is ours," the man said, pointing to the only car sitting on its tires. Its roof was smashed.

"Looks like it got rolled totally over," said Massey, packing up the first aid kit again and snapping off his plastic gloves.

"I guess," said the man, shifting his hold on his wife.

"I called the ambulance," Massey said. "Is there anywhere you can go after she sees an EMT?"

"My daughter lives over in Eaton," he said. "Did it hit there too?"

"No," said Greg. Eaton was north of them. "Give me her number, and I'll try to get someone to call her, okay?"

The man couldn't remember the number. "It's on speed dial, you know? I should know it, but I don't."

"That's okay," Greg said, patting his shoulder. "She'll hear the news and find you, I'm sure." He hated to leave the couple, but they'd done what they could. Other people might need their help even more. Massey's work has stopped the woman's wound from gushing blood, and the EMTs would get here when they could.

He and Massey went together to check the wreck of the house across the street where the young family lived. As Greg climbed a pile of lumber, it began to slide under him. The horrible thought that he might be climbing over dead children hit him, and he felt sickened by the thought of a baby's delicate skin being torn by the board skidding under him. He leaned forward and had to slap his hands down to keep his balance.

A nail jabbed his palm, and he yanked that hand back. The boards quit sliding and he stood up. Falling on a bunch of protruding nails could put him entirely out of commission. He'd have to be more careful.

"You okay, partner?" called Massey.

"Yeah," he said, wiping his palm on his pants. It was bleeding—and he'd probably need a tetanus shot—but he was fine. Belatedly, he pulled on the pink gardening gloves. "See anything?"

"No. Let me call again." He yelled a "hello" into the debris pile. No answer.

Greg turned and called across the street to the man with the injured wife. "Did this house have a basement?"

The man hesitated. "I think, yeah. They were all built at the same time, back in the 50s."

Greg said to Massey, "Maybe they got downstairs and are safe somewhere down there."

"Huh," he said. "Maybe." But he didn't sound as if he meant it.

"Let's spend another minute more looking around here, and then—" he hated to say it, but... "—we have to keep going, I guess." Again, Holly flashed into his mind. What if it were her down there? He pushed the thought aside. Getting emotional wouldn't make him do his job any better.

Massey bent over to pick up a blue plaid flannel shirt, held it up, balled it up and shoved it in his back pocket.

"Uh, Massey, you need an extra shirt?"

"It's not for me. The guy across the street. It could get cold tonight, and who knows where he'll end up. Whoever's this was isn't going to miss it that much."

He made his way carefully around the debris pile, looking for any sign of life—or death. He was in a pile of lumber and pipes, all straight lines, except for one thing. "Wait." Maybe it was just a bunched up sweater or something. He leaned over and picked it up—it was a mud-streaked little dog. Dead. "It's black," he said, holding it up to show Massey. "Under the mud, I can see black curly hair."

"Oh, little Winkie. You think?"

"Tinker," corrected Greg. "Might well be him. Poor thing." A ragged chunk of lumber had been driven into the dog's head, right above the eyes, like a purposeful kill shot. His back was broken too, Greg thought. Hard to tell which injury had killed him.

"Leave it."

"I'll at least take it out to the sidewalk by the car, so she has a better chance of finding it."

"If you insist," said Massey. "Dogs," he said in disgust.

"We need dogs," said Greg.

"Not the time for a philosophical discussion about pets, bud," said Massey.

"No, I didn't mean it that way. I'm thinking, we could use some search and rescue dogs for these totaled homes." And tomorrow, they'd need cadaver dogs. He kicked at a loose sheet of plywood, catching it with his toe and turning it over. Nothing beneath.

"Yeah, I get you. Dogs would be helpful." Massey stood up from where he'd been squatting and shining his flashlight under a pile of debris. I'm not hearing anything, and I can't see anything, and maybe this family wasn't even home. Let's go on."

They stopped again at the couple. Massey handed over the shirt to the man and reassured them that help would be coming.

"Thank you."

Greg bent down to look at the woman, who was pale. "She doing okay?"

The eyes fluttered open. "I'll be fine," she said.

"Of course you will," he said.

Back at the car, he dropped Tinker's corpse onto the sidewalk. From the first aid kit, he grabbed a bandage and antibiotic cream out of the first aid kit and bandaged his palm. Then he radioed in again. The first raindrop hit the windshield, and then many more.

"How's the rescue of the chief and everyone else going?" he asked Dispatch.

"They've just got the equipment set up and started working on it. No time estimate yet, even. Oh, and you didn't hear, I expect. Magarelli and Simms reported in."

"They're okay?" Greg was relieved.

"Yeah. They were involved in a situation that kept them off-air, but they're fine."

Greg was curious, but there was no time for gossip. "Good to hear. Any new orders?"

"No. Chief Stephens said she'd assign their car to downtown, and for the rest of you to keep patrolling as planned."

And so they did. The next street gave them their first bodies. Neighbors from the houses just outside the tornado's path had helped rescue a young family just inside it. A woman was alive, but a thin man was dead, along with a boy not far from Holly's age.

A neighbor was trying to comfort the woman, who was

sobbing and keening over the child's body. The neighbor looked up when Greg and Massey approached. "They homeschooled," she said. "So everybody was home when it hit."

Greg wondered who worked in the family, if both parents were home all day. He bent to check the man's pulse at his neck, but he felt nothing. This guy wouldn't be working again, in any case. He could feel the moment of cold cynicism that swept over him whenever he confronted death. He knew it for what it was, a defense mechanism, but he worried that one day it'd sweep over him, hard and prickly and dark, and never leave him, changing him into a person he didn't want to become.

The rain started coming down in earnest as they finished checking the street, soaking the living and dead and rescuers alike.

They got in the car and drove to the next street. Massey got out of the car, trotted forward, called, "Hey!"

Greg looked up and saw him staring south. He stood and put his hand on his gun, expecting trouble.

But it was just the two officers patrolling the south side, visible a block away. Between them was a no man's land of destruction.

Massey waded into it partway and called, "How's downtown look?"

Higgins yelled, "Totaled for about six blocks east of here. West of here, it missed Main."

The rain came down harder and he could no longer see them down there. Massey turned to the destroyed houses on the opposite side, and Greg took this side. They found three more bodies, mud-covered, unidentifiable, the biggest one's face smashed beyond recognition.

"For all I know it could be my best friend," said Greg.

"Your best friend live around here?"

"No, I meant—I can barely tell that it's a white-skinned person. ID is going to be hard."

"White male." Massey lifted the corpse's left hand and wiped away some mud. "No wedding band." He let the arm fall, and it hit a piece of aluminum with a twang.

"Christ. You have triage tags in that first aid kit?"

"Yeah. Here." He handed Greg a wad of black strips, and Greg bent to tag all three bodies. They would be visiting his dreams in the coming weeks.

On the next street, they found a green sedan lying on its side, badly dented. One side of it had most of the paint scoured off.

"You think it's from back there?" Greg said. "Where the injured woman was? Remember, the young family?"

"Could be any green car."

"Still." Greg thought of Holly. What if her body was buried in rubble back there? What if she could still be saved? He'd want someone to be working on finding her.

"You smell gas?" Massey said.

Greg raised his nose like a retriever and sniffed. He could smell the sulfurous additive for natural gas. "Damn. Yeah. You have a wrench in the car?"

"Probably. I'll go look."

"I'll hunt for the street shutoff."

Easier said than done. The road was covered with debris. The shut-off for the street was going to be under a plate, flush with the sidewalk or street. Good luck finding it. He needed the exact location. He tried his radio and couldn't get Dispatch, but could get the patrol team to the south. They radioed in to Dispatch from their car and in a few minutes got him an address—in front of 147.

Massey was coming his way with a canvas bag of tools. "Wait," Greg called. "Read the address off that house." He pointed to the first one that still stood.

Massey went over and turned around, yelling, "124."

"The shut-off is back your way," he said. "In front of 147."

Massey turned and hunted for the right address.

Greg left him to it. His radio cracked at his hip, but he couldn't get a signal strong enough to hear the voice. He jogged back to the car.

Greg got Dispatch on the radio, and as soon as he identified himself, she said, "You need to find shelter."

"Why?"

"There's another tornado coming."

Chapter 8

Holly. Greg's first though was his daughter. "Are you sure about the tornado?"

"Yeah. They have confirmed sightings over in West County. The storm is tracking this way."

"That's impossible. It can't come right over the same place as the first, can it?"

"I guess it can. And Greg?"

"Yeah?"

"They're calling it a big wedge. I think it might be even worse than the first one."

"Christ, you haven't seen this damage yet. How could it possibly be worse?"

"People can see this one, at least. We've had six hysterical calls on 911."

"Thanks for the warning." He leaned over and hit the siren, quick, to get Massey's attention.

When the other man looked back, he half-stood from the car and waved him back, making the gesture urgent. Then he realized the city storm siren was out. No electricity, no siren. How would they warn people?

He got back on the radio. "You have an ETA for this thing?"

"Maybe ten minutes?"

He cut off the radio before he let out a profanity.

Massey trotted up. "I found a guy who knew how to shut the gas off and had a wrench. Now what's the rush?"

"We have another tornado coming, which may be bigger than the first. And less than ten minutes to get people—and ourselves—to safety."

"Hellfire." Massey dropped into the driver's seat and held his hand out. "Car keys," he snapped.

"You still have them."

Greg might be thinking selfishly, but he had more reason than the obvious personal one to make the suggestion he was about to make. "We should go back to the elementary school."

"To get your kid?"

"No, not just that. I'm thinking, how many people can we warn in ten minutes? How many can we save, best case? At least there we have a concentration of people we can help. Kids, teachers, maybe some parents. If we knock on doors on this street for five minutes, how many can we get downstairs before we have to quit? Five people? Ten? Yeah, of course I'm worried about Holly, but it's a matter of numbers."

Massey gave a curt nod. "Hopefully people in town have their radios on."

Greg knew not everyone was well-prepared for emergencies. He doubted half the people in town had battery-operated radios. Maybe one in twenty had a NOAA radio. Maybe far fewer. They might think their smartphones would get them online, but that wasn't happening now either, not with cell towers knocked down or overwhelmed with traffic. And some of the people with portable radios might be outside, helping people, cleaning up downed tree limbs, and not listening to the news.

And the town storm siren had no power.

That left nearly everyone without a warning. Not that being

prepared like the most extreme of preppers would have saved the people in the completely erased houses he'd been looking at the past half-hour.

And it was going to happen again.

Greg said, "We don't have any orders. If you don't have a better suggestion, I'll call in the plan."

"I guess it's best," said Massey, starting the car.

Greg got on the radio—the chief couldn't talk, so he told Dispatch where they were headed. "We can get the children we left there down into the basement, at least," he said.

"I'll pass that on," said the dispatcher.

Massey said, "Let me tell those people on this street." He backed up the car, yelled a warning to the grieving woman and her neighbors, and then tore out north, up the street to the north.

Greg fumbled the external speakers on and said, "Get to shelter. Tornado coming," over and over. He had no idea if anyone heard the message or not. He beeped the siren for a second and repeated the message as Massey turned them left, then right again onto Central.

With a screech of tires, Massey pulled into the drive that ran in front of the school, and they both got out, slamming their doors in unison. They sprinted up the front steps, and Massey peeled off to the left, saying, "I'll clear any rooms down here again."

Greg ran for the office. The receptionist was there, on the landline. "Another tornado," he shouted at her.

Her face went pale. "I—have to go," she said into the phone, then raised her face to Greg. "Not a joke?"

"No, not a joke. Can you make the announcement again?"

"There's no power!"

"Damn. How many people are here now?"

"Fifty, sixty?"

"In classrooms?"

"Downstairs in the cafeteria, some of them, but yes, some are in various rooms."

"I'm clearing the same wing I did earlier. You get everybody out of any offices, then run downstairs yourself."

"How long do we have?" she called as he ran out of the room.

"Five minutes, if you're lucky," he shouted back.

Greg ran down the familiar hallway, flinging doors open, classrooms and bathrooms both. The third classroom had ten children and two adults supervising them. "Get back downstairs, right now."

This time, no one fought him. They dropped everything and ran.

The fifth door had a teacher and four children—one of whom was Holly. "Let's get downstairs, everyone," he said. "Holly, get over here, now."

She sprung out of her chair and ran to him. He scooped her up in his arms and carried her along. "Just a couple more doors to check," he said to her. The children and teacher who had been with her passed them by, headed for the stairs. The art room had a few people in it, an adult and two kids playing on the floor with clay. He got them up and moving, and when everyone had passed through to the steps downstairs, he turned to yell a general warning to anyone he might have somehow missed.

"Tornado coming! Everybody downstairs right now!"

He went into the last west-facing room and jogged to the window to look at the sky. The rain had stopped. To the west, he could see it, a black patch growing in size. The first tornado had spanned about a half a block. This one was bigger. As it came closer, he froze in place, mesmerized, watching it grow and grow, filling more and more of the sky. It was huge. It was going to take out a swath two blocks wide. Maybe more.

And it was coming right this way.

Holding tight to his daughter, he ran out of the room and took the steps down as fast as safety allowed. As he came to the last child sitting in line in the hallway, he slid down to the ground, his arms wrapped tightly around Holly. "Put your legs around me, sweetie," he said. "Hold on to Dad."

There was complete quiet this time—no chattering children, no one shouting, just silent apprehension.

Outside, the wind began to scream.

Chapter 9

"Meek? You still okay?" said Adam.

"Same old me."

"Except you're not doing anything for a change. You're usually doing two things at once."

"Enforced rest period," she said. "Like in kindergarten. I hated them then too."

"I'm going to go call for help again."

She hated the seconds when he was gone. He had left three times now, and if he was keeping time as he said he was, leaving every five minutes, maybe twenty minutes had passed. She was starting to hurt more. One hip bone was pressed into the tile so hard, she knew she was bruised there, could imagine broken capillaries spreading from that point outward, like an illustration in her bio textbook.

"I'm back." Adam's voice came through the wall. "I got to talk to someone this time—a couple of guys, actually. They ran off to get help. There's a fire truck on campus."

"That's good." She cleared her throat. "I guess I'll be stuck for a while longer, though."

"I wish I could change that."

"You should call your mom. And mine, I guess—but don't

worry her if you do call." Her mother didn't handle stress well.

"The phones are out. The electricity too."

"I guess my mother will be coming to check on me." She realized then that she wasn't the only one in trouble. "Unless the tornado got her too."

"I'm sure she's fine."

"What about your family, Adam?"

"I don't know."

"You should go find out. You've told someone, now. I'll get rescued." It killed her to say it. She didn't *want* him to go. "You need to go home and check on your brother and sister, and let your mom know you're okay."

"The school isn't badly damaged. Just the parking lot and stadium. If they hear that, they'll assume I'm fine."

"The stadium? Was anyone out on the track?"

"I don't know. It was raining, so maybe they'd all gone in, or had gym inside last period."

"I hope so. I hope I'm the only person hurt in the whole town."

"Are you? Hurt bad, do you think?"

"I don't know. I—" She hated to think about it, but she wanted to tell him too. "I can't feel my legs, Adam. Not at all."

"Meek," he said. Nothing more, just her name, worry and care and sympathy in the tone, coming through the tumbled spaces and trying to touch her, to reassure her.

"You're a good guy, Adam. I hope you know that."

"Then why did you dump me, Meek? If I'm that good a guy?"

"Do we need to talk about this now?"

"I want to."

"Oh? I don't."

He laughed bitterly. "Don't I know it. But you can't run away from me, for once. Tell me."

"I told you that I wanted to focus on my schoolwork. I'm not ready for something serious."

"Then we can have something less serious." He hesitated. "If you don't hate me."

"I don't hate you. Not a bit."

There were long seconds of silence. Malika could hear sirens in the distance. The lines of light she could see were getting brighter. "Is the sun coming out?"

"Was it sex, Meek? I didn't push you, did I?"

"No." In a way, of course, it was sex. "I was as interested in that as you." She surely hoped no one was eavesdropping on this conversation.

"Was it that the sex wasn't—" he cleared his throat "—any good? Did I disappoint you?"

"No, Adam. You didn't disappoint me."

"You didn't disappoint me, either. I mean, it was nice. I didn't hurt you at all? Physically?"

"No." He had been her first, but it hadn't hurt one bit. It was clumsy the first time, but that was her fault as much as his— maybe even more her fault. She had been nervous—had had stage fright, without being on stage. But by the third time, she was mostly over that, and it was just her and Adam, moving slower by then, which was even nicer. It seemed like a natural part of their caring for each other. When he looked into her eyes after she had come the first time, it was like religion, like the touch of God in her heart. She felt as big as the universe and, at the same time, in a tiny, private cocoon of two, the only two people fully alive in the world right then.

"Meek?"

"Yeah," she said, coming back to the present from the bittersweet memory.

"I didn't hurt you?"

"Not at all."

"Then why? Don't give me that story about schoolwork. That wasn't it, was it?"

"It wasn't."

"Tell me."

What if, Malika thought, she died? What if no one got to her in time? What if the whole building collapsed on her? What if they came and got her, and something in her was hurt so badly that she didn't make it? Would she want him wondering for months or years, or believing the lie she had told him?

"Was it another guy? You haven't been with anyone else since, cuz I've been paying attention, but was it that you fell in—"

"I was pregnant." It was out of her mouth before she could stop herself. "I was pregnant and had an abortion."

Nothing.

"Adam?"

Nothing.

More insistent. "Adam!"

His voice was soft. "Give me a second."

She waited several seconds, but she couldn't stay quiet. "*Say something.*"

"I—I gotta go check and see where those rescuers are."

She heard him walk away. And wondered if he'd ever be back. *I shouldn't have told him.*

* * *

"They're coming." Long minutes passed, and Malika tried not to think at all—not about her legs or Adam or the abortion or anything.

"Adam?"

"Yeah. There's a wrecker and fire truck in the lot now. They're going to pull the bus out, if they can do it without hurting you. And they want me out of here."

"Thank you. You're being very nice."

"I love you, Malika. I'm not nice, I'm just...stupid, I guess." He heaved a sigh. "And so mad at you right now I'm glad I can't get to you. I never ever thought I'd hit a girl, but I want to shake you until your teeth rattle."

"I knew you wouldn't like if I did it. That's why I didn't—"

"Not for that. Geez, Meek, I wouldn't want to hurt you because of that. It's for not telling me right then. For not trusting me. I'm angry about *that*, you fool." He took a breath. "The fire guys just told me to come outside again. They don't want anyone else in here in case something else falls down from the ceiling."

"Okay."

"I just.... I'll see you later."

"Sure, see you sometime."

"I'll be right *here*. When they get you out, I'm going to be right here, Meek. You think I stopped loving you in like five minutes? Jesus, you're an idiot. For someone so smart, you sure are stupid sometimes." With that, he was gone.

* * *

"Miss?" A man's voice from outside. "Malika, is it? You in there? Awake?"

"Yes," she said.

"Your friend says you can't move your legs."

"I don't know if they're pinned or paralyzed or what," she said.

"Okay. We're going to get you out. It may take a few minutes, so you just hold tight."

She heard a truck engine approaching, and then the beep-beep of a back-up signal started. A pause. Then voices, shouting—she couldn't hear what. And a metallic clunk. More voices, or the same ones. Every second felt like ten minutes. She wanted out of here, and wanted it worse now that they were here to help her.

Though she didn't really want to see Adam face to face. She had never meant to tell him, not ever. She thought she would move on with her life, and the memory of him and the pregnancy—which she still couldn't believe had happened, they had been so careful—and the abortion, paid for with her own savings from work. The trip to Columbus on the bus, and the trip back, cramping, more relieved than guilty and then more guilty because of the relief, and holding the secret inside herself. Her mother wouldn't have disapproved, but Malika didn't tell her. Her pastor probably would have understood her reasons. And now, it seemed, even Adam would have.

She was so used to doing everything on her own. Her brother and sister weren't much use. Her mother wasn't. Everything had been up to Malika for a long time. She had thought taking care of the pregnancy would be too. And she had gotten through it. She had no regrets.

But it would have been nice to have someone to talk it over with. Someone to hold her hand on the bus ride, maybe.

"Slow down, now!" a voice shouted outside. She heard grinding, and a big pop, as they started to do whatever it was they were doing out there.

"It's coming," said a different voice.

"Hold up!" the first voice said. "Miss? Malika, you okay in there? Anything fall on you?"

"Nothing moved at all," she yelled back.

"Pull 'er forward," he called again.

This time, the light changed. Malika couldn't see behind her, but she could tell that something was moving away, letting in more light.

With a banging, steely clank, something fell, and she yelped in fear.

"Stop!" shouted the voice. "You okay?"

"I'm sorry. It just scared me. Nothing hurt me."

"You sure?"

"I'm sure." She still couldn't feel anything below her hips.

The engine outside—louder now—ground gears and revved again. Creaking, groaning, snapping noises. A thud. More and more light filtering in.

For the first time since she had woken, she felt hope. They

were going to get her out of here. Maybe nothing would be wrong with her. If her legs were hurt, she'd deal with it.

"Okay," yelled the voice. "Haul it over there to the other wrecks." Then the engine sound was gone and two voices were talking together, more quietly, so she could only hear the murmur of it.

"Okay, Malika?" the first voice called in. "You still okay?"

"Still okay," she said. Just hurry up!

"We're going to winch up a beam here, and I want you to scream really loud if anything hurts you, okay?"

"Okay."

"We're going to move as fast as we can."

"Thank you, sir," she called back.

There was a different engine noise, and a motor on top of that, and some squealing. Long seconds ticked off. Then more squealing, and the light changed again. And rain came down on her.

She laughed at it. Maybe a little hysterically, but those raindrops meant the roof was coming off her, and that was good.

The noise quieted, and the voice came back. "Still good?"

"Great," she said.

"Atta girl." The squealing started again and she felt—blessedly felt—something lift off her. It lifted more.

Then blood began to flow into her legs, and they started to hurt.

She forgot her moment of toughness about being a brave patient, fighting off some crippling injury, soldiering on, no matter what. She forgot about school and her plans for university and Adam and everything. As the pressure lifted, the pain increased. And kept building, and kept on. And it went way beyond the cramps from the abortion, and way beyond the broken ulna she'd had at age nine, and way beyond anything she knew a human being could endure.

She would have started screaming, but the pain was so great

now that it stole her breath away.

"Okay," shouted the man. "I can see her." The voice came as if from a mile off, or through a pillow covering her ears. "Malika, you okay?"

She tried to answer, but the pain wouldn't let her. It was a dragon, teeth clamping her legs, rending them, trying to rip them off and steal them. And it had stolen her ability to breathe too.

"Okay. I got it," said the voice to someone else. "Take this one too, and I think I can get to her."

She heard the words as a series of sounds, but they made little sense to her. The pain had worked its way all the way down to her toes now, and her legs felt about ten feet long, pain every millimeter of the way. She gasped, and finally a breath came, and when it came out, it was a scream.

"Meek!" It was Adam.

"Get back, son," the second voice said. "We'll get her out."

A third male voice, panting for air, said, "There's another tornado coming."

Good, thought Malika, as her air ran out and the scream—like someone else's scream, she had so little control over it—dwindled away with her breath. Good, let another tornado come and kill me. I don't want to live with this kind of pain. Not one more second. *Jesus, please, take me now.*

* * *

She must have blacked out for a few seconds—not fainted, but just...gone away, in her mind. When she came fully to herself again, the first thing she heard was Adam, yelling at someone.

That was wrong. Adam never yelled.

Her legs still hurt, like *blazes*. Yes, literally like blazes, hot fire licking up and down them. Like her legs had gone to Hell while the rest of her remained on Earth. And rats with burning little claws were skittering up and down them. But she wasn't screaming now. That was good. It'd just upset everyone. She managed a whisper. "Save me, Jesus."

"Get this winched up," said the second man. "Son, get back. I'm not telling you again."

"Meek, are you in there?" Adam.

"I'm—" She gasped for breath. "Here." Then the pain welled again, and she bit her lips together to keep from screaming again. A moan escaped through her nose. She had no idea a person could hurt like this. It was a revelation, and one she'd never forget.

Another squeal from the equipment outdoors, and then something else moved, and her shoulders were free too. She reached a hand back, feeling the back of her neck. But no, she didn't have to worry about paralysis any more. Heck, she'd *welcome* paralysis now. Anything to make her legs stop burning.

Crunching sounds behind her. She tried to lever herself up onto one elbow.

"No, hon," a man said, the first voice. "Lie still. Let us do the work."

Adam's voice: "She sucks at letting anyone else help her."

She felt the strange man's hands touch her head, her ears, her neck, moving down over her shoulders.

"My arms—fine," she managed to say, raising one hand to prove it.

"Okay, but I'll check you out here. Just stay still and let me see."

"It's my legs," she hissed.

"They hurt?"

She nodded, then realized he might not be able to see it. "They hurt bad," she said.

"I'll try and be gentle." Fingers probed her thighs. It didn't hurt any worse. The pain was all coming from inside her, and nothing he did made it flare up. He lightly squeezed an ankle over her shoe. "You feel that?"

"Yeah," she said. She realized tears were dripping off her nose.

Stupid. Crying wouldn't solve a thing. She sniffed and willed the tears to stop.

"Your legs feeling any better?"

She thought about it. "I'm not screaming now," was as far as she was willing to go. And she could think more clearly. For a minute there, when her legs were first released, the pain had kept her mind from working right.

"It'll probably hurt more when we move you."

She remembered what she had just heard. "A tornado?" she said. "A different one?"

"There's another coming, yeah. But we're pretty sure it'll be a bit north of here this time."

"Tell Adam," she said, and then the pain heated up, and she had to pant and catch her breath before finishing the thought. "Tell him to get away." Just in case they were wrong.

"The kid, he's really worried about you. That's your boyfriend?"

"Yes." It was easier than explaining their whole history. "Tell him to go. A basement."

"Okay," the man said. "Hold tight one second. I just need to check something out here."

She could hear three of them talking. She wondered about a second tornado. Was that even possible, for two tornados to hit the same place within an hour? She'd never heard of it. Maybe it was a mistake, like the warning coming too late. She hoped that was all it was.

"They think we're in a safe area," said the man, coming back to her side. She heard someone else walking nearer. "We have a stretcher here. We're going to get you on it, and it'll probably hurt."

"Okay," she said.

She tried to relax, let go, and let them move her as they needed to. It did hurt. Her legs felt like burning iron rods attached to her hips, still. But it wasn't as awful, not *quite* as bad as it had been when they unpinned her and she first felt them.

They got her onto the stretcher, still face-down, and then they attached something to its sides with a metallic snap. The first man stayed while the second stepped back. The squealing noise again, and the stretcher was being lifted, the man with her balancing it as it started to sway. "Go up," he called over his shoulder. She could see his arm move as he signaled behind him. Then the stretcher got raised more, and it was about at his waist level. He guided it as it swung out, and she could see, as she moved over them, a toilet on its side, and a pile of crushed black stall walls, and then lumber and bricks, and then she was hanging out over the tarmac of the parking lot, with scattered glass and bent chrome and stuff all over it. What a mess. Somebody needed to clean that up.

The uniformed firefighters—she could see the truck now in her peripheral vision, a medium-sized fire truck with ladders and hoses and all that—got her stretcher up onto their truck and strapped her in, way up high. When they moved away, she could see out over the roofs. And she could see the tornado too. It was in the distance—she couldn't tell how far away, and going from left to right. She could see all kinds of things blowing around it— a whole roof, big sheets of something—metal or house walls, and thousands of smaller bits that could be anything.

Maybe even people.

"Is it coming this way?" she asked the firefighter.

"Thank God, no," he said. "We're driving you to the evacuation point, south of here. You'll be in a hospital in Cincinnati within an hour, and well away from the storms."

Adam was in front of her face, squatting down. "You're out. It'll be okay now."

The fireman was telling him to get the hell off the truck.

"Thank you," she said to Adam, who hadn't budged. "Thank them, and anyone who helped."

"I will. They'll take care of you. And I'll be there—at the hospital—as soon as I can, okay? I'll tell your mom too, bring her with me, and my mom too."

"Adam." She ran out of words, so simply extended her hand, and he gave her his. It was warm. She pulled it in and kissed his knuckles.

Chapter 10

It's up to me. Sherryl went back into Jim's room, and stared, amazed, at the damage. The walls, when they had fallen, had scattered bits of themselves all around. The dresser had pushed itself into the next room to the left, leaving a space on the floor with less debris. She ducked around fallen wires, hoping the electricity was off, but being careful anyway not to touch them.

Glass crunched underfoot. She smelled lumber, the scent as strong as it'd be out back of a lumber yard, of freshly sawed wood. Stopping at a tumble of bent and cracked beams—or were they joists?—she called out for her husband. "Jim?"

No sound.

At least the bed wasn't crushed. That gave her hope. Best case, it had protected him from flying glass.

Worst case, it had rolled on top of him and was pressing down on him right now.

The thought made her move. She leaned over—her back twanged again—and bent her knees, trying to lift a chunk of drywall out of the way so she could see better. Her knees popped as she tried to lift. Instead of coming straight up, it pivoted around one corner. She yanked her end back toward her, uncovering a broken table lamp base. And a bony ankle, sticking out of blue striped pajamas.

"Jim," she said. "Can you hear me?"

No answer.

Her heart hammering in her chest, she leaned over, grabbing the end of the bed for balance. Trying to not put any weight on it, she leaned over. There was his leg, from the knee down, pointed this way. No blood on it. As she bent down, a second leg came into view, under the bed, shadowed by it.

She could smell urine. He wore diapers, of course. This one needed changing. It was a minor problem. Was he alive?

"Jim!" she said. "Talk to me."

Still nothing.

Okay, the bed didn't seem to be on him. It was covered with broken glass, though. She picked up a broken chunk of wood and swept glass off the bare mattress. Then she tugged her sleeve down over her hand and plucked off the last shards. She lifted a leg as far as she could—not far enough, so maybe she should take up yoga or something—and put it back down. Okay, then, just sort of *throw* yourself onto the bed.

She looked first, making sure she wasn't pressing down on Jim, then she gave it her best long-jump effort, which at this age was more like a short jump. But her top half was on the bed.

Ouch. She hadn't gotten every piece of glass. She wriggled her way forward until she could flip over, then checked her shoulder where she'd felt a stab of pain. Blood seeped out. She slid her hand over and, when the hurt sharpened, knew she had found it. With her nails—cut short for gardening, damn it—she picked and picked and finally got the bit of glass out. Not even an inch long. She flicked it over the far side of the bed, and watched as fresh blood welled into the fabric of her blouse.

I'll live, she thought, dismissing the blood. Brushing at the mattress again, she made her way forward until she could lean down and look under the bed. She couldn't see Jim's face. It was hidden by the fallen wall. But the bed had broken the force of the wall falling.

Her back hurt, and she wasn't strong enough to push the section of wall away. But maybe her legs would do it. They were stronger. Pivoting around, she got her feet under the edge of the bit of drywall over the bed and tried to push it away.

Nothing.

Okay. More leverage. She wriggled her hips down *farther* so her knees were bent more. Then she grasped the material of the mattress ticking itself, held on, and pushed from her thighs. The drywall moved maybe an inch, and she repositioned her feet to get more surface pressure and *pushhhhed*.

No more movement. After ten or fifteen seconds of futile effort, she quit, and panted, feeling her heart pound.

Don't have a heart attack doing this. Somehow, I doubt you'll be found very soon if you do.

The section of drywall must be held in place by something she couldn't see.

She tried to remember what had been right there, next to the bed. A bedside table. Small lamp. Tissues, water glass.

She rolled over to the side of the bed and reached as far under the debris as she could, trying to find a pulse, or movement, or anything that could reassure her that Jim was alive. But there was something in the way.

Was his chest crushed? His head? She could feel tears pushing behind her eyes, but she refused to let herself cry. Get him out first. Or at least figure out if he's hurt. Then fall apart.

"Jim," she said again. "Answer me, dammit."

Again, no reply.

Okay, so get back over to the other side of the bed, and look in from the closet end. She surveyed the fallen wall. It was cracked into three big pieces, and a few smaller ones. Maybe she could crawl over that one, and peek down under and see him. Maybe.

Nothing else to do but try it.

Or—wait. It was just drywall. Maybe she could punch a hole

in it here, over the space next to the bed.

With what?

Not the closet door—too big. There had to be something. Sherryl scooted back off the foot of the bed and retraced her steps, this time kicking through the debris, looking for something dense, sharp, like a weapon. There was a thin blonde piece of molding— too brittle. So something in the closet?

She picked her way over there and found a 2-by-4, with nails protruding from it. Problem was, it was long, and buried under something. She tried to pull it out, to no avail. Could she break it? No. Too sturdy. The closet—was there anything in there? She checked.

Hangers? Plastic ones only. A shoe? Not hard enough. Her slacks tore on the edge of the smashed-up closet door. No matter. At the back of the closet, she pawed around and her hands found a possible weapon to attack the drywall with. An umbrella—not one of the new, shorter, fold-up models, but an older sort, with a metal tip.

Maybe.

She twisted and tugged at it until it popped free, and hurried back over to the bed. Kneeling on the side, she began jabbing at the fallen wall. The drywall gave easily. But there was something else in there with a plastic mesh, and it was tough stuff.

"Dammit," she cried. This was taking far too long. "Jim, are you hearing me?"

She heard, very softly, just under where she had been aiming her umbrella, a weak cough.

"Jimmy! Jimmy! It's me!"

Nothing more from him.

She punched away more drywall, and finally there was a hole big enough to push her hands into. Putting the umbrella on the mattress, careful not to lose it, she reached in and began clawing at the plastic. It was really tough.

There was plenty of broken glass. Maybe she could slice it.

It took her two minutes of pawing around the floor on the other side of the bed to find a bit of window glass still attached to the frame. Her hands were cut in a half-dozen places by now, but she could hold this piece of glass by the wood bit.

She began hacking at the plastic. Sawing at it. Attacking it. Finally, she got a piece to cut, and she began to change her technique, trying to repeat what she had done, getting more cut, adapting her technique more, and the plastic began to spring away from the hole. She pulled at that until she had a hole through the wall.

Then she leaned over to see beneath—but it was too dark. She needed a bigger hole.

Back to the umbrella, furiously slamming it down into the drywall, working faster now, feeling like time was running out, she slowly widened the hole.

She pressed her mouth to it. "Jim!" she said. "Can you hear me?"

"Sher?" she heard.

Relief flooded her. "It's me, it's me."

"What?" She could hear him breathing, shallow raspy breaths. "What happened?"

"We had a tornado."

"I can't breathe," he said.

"I'll get you out," she promised. But she didn't see how. Maybe a crane, or chainsaws, or something like that could get him out.

But there was only her, one frightened old woman. She turned around and screamed toward the hallway, "Someone help me!"

But no one came. She didn't expect anyone to.

She began widening the hole again, umbrella, then glass, then umbrella tip, then cutting more, until the hole was as large as her head.

She leaned forward as far as she dared. She didn't want to overbalance and fall onto whatever had him pinned in there. "Are you hurt?"

"Yeah," he said. "Are we home, or in the nursing home?"

"The nursing home," she said.

"I'm sorry, honey."

"You have nothing to be sorry for. It's just a tornado, a storm. Not your fault."

"I'm sorry I'm sick."

"Oh, Jim." The tears threatened again. "That's not your fault either."

"I said something to hurt you today, I think."

"No," she said. "You didn't."

"I know I do. I don't want to. And I can't ever remember what I've said, not for long. But I see your face."

Her eyes were adjusting to the dim light. What she saw shocked her. There was a heavy board, like a roof beam, and the bedside table canted over, and all of it on Jim's chest. "I wish I could see your face right now."

"I can see yours—or part of it."

She reached down and cautiously tried to find some part of him to touch. There. She felt his pajamas, moved her hand, felt the board. Moved along the board, up as far as she could reach.

"Hurts," he said.

"I'm sorry." She drew her hand back, felt the moisture, and pulled her head out of the dimness to look at her hand.

Blood.

Her stomach turned over. He was injured. He was pinned. He was a frail old man, and there was no one to help get him out. She pushed her face back into the hole she had made in the drywall. "How bad does it hurt?"

"I've felt better." His tone was wry.

It was like the old Jim, and it was nice to have him back. She didn't know for how long, though. Soon enough, he'd fade back into the fog of the disease.

"You know how much I love you?" she said.

"I do. And I love you too. Even when I'm...what this makes me, mean and confused. The bit that's really me, that bit loves you fiercely." Then he started coughing. She could hear the pain in it.

"I need to get you help."

"No."

"I won't leave you for long, I promise."

"I don't want help."

"Jim, don't be—"

"Shut up, and let me say this while I can think. I don't want anyone to save me. I want to die. I want to stop being a burden on you."

"You won't die. You have years yet."

"I don't want them. Not like this."

She knew he didn't. When he'd been diagnosed, two years ago, he'd said so. He'd thought of killing himself then. But she had talked him out of it. "I can't just...."

"You can. I'm tasting blood, and I think—" He started coughing again. "I think maybe I'm hurt bad enough that, if you leave me be for an hour or two, that might be the end of it."

She couldn't. She couldn't just leave him to die. "It'll hurt."

"Not for long, I think."

She reached back in to touch him, just her fingertips. "Don't ask me to do this."

"All you have to do is nothing. Please."

She stayed silent, listening to his labored breathing. It seemed worse now.

He coughed again, weakly.

When he had talked about killing himself, she had begged him to stay. Maybe they'll find a treatment. Maybe it'll go slow with you. Maybe we'll have some great months. She had argued hard, and argued unfairly at the end, asking if he wanted her to find his body, or to maybe get arrested for murder. He had begged her to, but she had refused to let him go.

And if it were just her—if the Alzheimer's was only hard on her—she'd known she could tough it out. If it took two more years or five, she'd stick with him. She'd thought as he got worse that he'd not notice any more, that the only person who would be unhappy about his growing dementia would be her.

But that wasn't how it had worked out. As he slid in and out of lucidity, he did know. What if they all knew? What if they were locked inside their minds, all of them, right up until the end, the true selves wanting to scream and beg for release from such a prison?

Who could say?

He coughed again, a pitiful sound.

She backed away and sent up a prayer. "God, tell me what to do. Send help, show me a sign. Tell me."

She heard footsteps outside in the hall, crunching through the debris, moving quickly. She turned as an orderly's head poked in.

"Ma'am," he said. "There's another tornado coming. You need to get to shelter."

"My husband," she said, pointing to the fallen wall.

"When it's gone by, we'll get him help. There's no time now. You have to run, get somewhere safer."

"Where?" she said, but he was gone. *That's the sign.* Not the one she wanted, but it was undeniably a sign.

She leaned forward again. "Jim?"

No answer.

"I will always love you. Always."

And then she did the hardest thing she had ever done, harder even than leaving Jim here that first night, which had been plenty hard.

Sherryl crawled back off the bed. She patted her pockets—the car keys were there. Her bag was somewhere under the debris. She left it, and Jim, and the room. And then she ran as fast as her aching old bones would take her, back up the hall.

Captain T

It's hard to believe, but without chasing at all, we're getting a second tornado, right in this same patch of Ohio. In fact, it looks like it could hit the same little town. We're rushing back west, going around the hook echo, and then sneaking up on it from the south, hoping to get some good shots.

Now that's a classic supercell structure. Look, we have a tail cloud and a wall cloud and—well, no. The whole wall cloud is the tornado. It must have formed a few miles back to grow to this size now. It's a huge wedge. Huge. Massive. Gotta be a quarter-mile wide.

Okay, look. Wow. Multiple vortices. Push in on one, Felix. There, you see it? If Felix can pull back, you should look for three—no, four more, dancing around. They're swarming around the central tornado, like bees around the hive.

I'm slowing down, checking my roads. I do not want to get caught too close to this one. It's a killer. Hoping it doesn't turn our way, and I want lots of choices for direction of escape. This next crossroads, and we'll jump out for a minute.

Hell yeah, I'm leaving the car running. Captain T is no fool.

Don't try this at home, people. Look at this massive tornado. Awesome. Nice lightning strike up ahead of it, if you didn't see that.

Whoa! Wait, buddy! See that truck passing me? Do not do that. People, if you pass an experienced storm chaser, see the Doppler on his truck, don't get any closer than he is to a tornado. In fact, stay well behind him, like a mile behind, that's my advice to you, fans.

A car is moving to the west on the crossroads here. Told them to keep going west. And then get into shelter, just in case. Tornados don't often circle around, but it has happened. And from what the radar tells us, there are more storms coming all evening. Doesn't seem fair to these people in Southwest Ohio, but there it is. You can't control Mother Nature.

Chapter 11

Sherryl felt tied to that room, to Jim pinned under the collapsed wall, and as she ran away, it felt like she was on an elastic band that wanted to pull her back.

But she made herself move forward. The central area behind the reception desk was full of glass. Many residents were in their wheelchairs, stuck in place but unharmed. Staff members rushed past, yelling to each other about the second tornado.

The receptionist was still sitting in her chair. It would be so easy to lean over, say, "My husband is pinned." And then let Fate decide—if rescuers got to him in time, that would be the decision. If they did not, then that was meant to be.

But she had promised him that she'd let him go.

If she walked out now without a word, would the guilt haunt her forever?

Quit thinking of yourself.

Jim was who mattered. And Jim didn't want to be rescued, or resuscitated. He wanted her to let him go.

She took a deep breath, stepped past the receptionist without a word, and pushed out the emergency exit door. *Keep walking.*

The parking lot had only taken the edge of the twister. Some cars had been spun around, out of their spots. Others had been pushed into one another. But her car was right where she left it. She jogged over, her back aching, her knees and hips feeling the extra strain.

Problem was, she could no longer back up her car. A pair of compact cars had been pushed forward just enough to block the drive. Well, screw it. She beeped open the car, got in, and started it. She bumped over the short concrete barrier, then down over the manicured lawn, the sidewalk, and drove onto the street.

She turned west on a side road. It ended at a T near the edge of town, and as she stopped, she could see the tornado. It was moving from her left to her right. Less than a mile away. Coming this way?

Mesmerized, she watched it flowing along the landscape. A pair of small twisters danced around it. A bright flash below the dark cloud startled her out of her hypnosis. That was probably a transformer blowing, out at the west side of town.

But it looked like it wasn't coming this way.

Go back to Jim.

The voice came clear as if someone were sitting right beside her in the car and saying it. She would respect his wishes and not call anyone in to help. She didn't think anyone would come in and force help on him. But she could lie on the bed, say nothing, and put her hand on him. She'd wait with him until there was no more movement.

And then get on with the rest of her life. Grieve, yes, but move on. She'd been grieving him for years already, truth be told. And when Jim was gone, she could help in town. There were people who'd need help after the storm. What could she do for them?

Suddenly, all the normal questions she should have been having flowed into her mind. Had her home survived? Greg and Holly? Her mah-jongg buddies and her neighbors? The Methodist church she belonged to? Schools? Downtown?

There would be a thousand things she might do around town, even if her own house had made it. It would keep her busy, distract her from her grief and guilt.

She made a left, and a left again, and drove back to the nursing home. No one should have to die alone.

* * *

Malika Landers was watching the tornado too, as the fire truck pulled out, sirens blaring. She prayed Adam would get somewhere safe, down into a basement. The truck turned a corner and she lost sight of the tornado.

The firefighter by her side was on the radio, and signed off before focusing again on her. "Okay, hon—what's your name again?"

She told him.

"Okay, Malika, we're going to give you some painkiller now, doctor says. You allergic to anything?"

"Nothing. But I think it hurts less now. Maybe if we just wait—"

"No, there's no reason to be stoic about it. Let's just chase all that pain off into the next county."

"Okay," she said, relieved she hadn't talked him out of it. She watched him scrub at the back of her hand with a swab, and then looked away as he pushed a needle in. Almost instantly, she felt a fuzzy cloud sweep over her, turning her thoughts and sensations into little bunches of soft moths that fluttered around, never finding a place to land. She felt pressure behind her eyes—not quite like tears trying to come out, but akin to that feeling—and she suspected it was the drug doing something to the pressure of fluids in her eyes. She tried to come up with a scientific explanation for the feeling, but her mind wasn't working well enough. Her lids fell, and she slipped into a dreamy state, where her legs didn't hurt much at all.

She spun like a dancer across a ballroom floor, dizzy and happy. Happy but sad. The phrase began to repeat in her mind.

Happy but sad, happy but sad. It made a waltz, she thought, as she faded into unconsciousness. Happy but sad.

* * *

Greg could hear it coming. Everyone in the school basement could. The wind was a scream, a warning siren itself, and with that came a low sound that pulsed like a bass beat oozing from an approaching car. He felt it in his thighs. Heard it. There was a taste of ozone in the air.

The wind noise grew, a roaring that hit all notes at once, high and low and everywhere in between. He heard a crash, a deep thud as something hit the wall of the school. In his mind's eye, he could see the debris cloud slamming bits of trash into the roof and walls.

The storm was already so loud, he wished he could cover his ears. Many of the children were doing just that. It struck him that a few people would lose some hearing today—it was that loud. Maybe, for children, it'd come back eventually. If they all survived the storm.

That was becoming less and less certain with every passing second.

As the sound grew, the shuddering motion of the building increased.

"Daddy," said Holly. "I'm scared."

He could barely hear her. "I know."

"Make it stop!"

He held her tighter. "Just don't let go of me. No matter what happens, don't let go."

She buried her face in his neck and nodded.

The wind's noise was like nothing he had heard before. He remembered what the fellow had said—no, not like a train. Like what? Wind. It was wind, but like a hard wind that whistles in your car window times ten thousand. It screamed, it moaned. It shook everything, harder and harder, until his vision started to blur with the movement of the walls.

A tremendous crash. At the far end of the hall, he could see acoustical tiles falling, one, then another, then another. He would have warned the kids to cover their heads, but they couldn't hear him yell. Another rending crash, and more tiles fell all at once. And then there was a rent in the ceiling and he could see light pouring through.

With a snap, something cracked right over his head. He bent over Holly the best he could and turned his head toward the far end of the hallway.

Like a zipper opening, the roof above their heads began to open. When it was a quarter of the way down the hall to him and Holly, he could see above, to the outside, to a black cloud of dirt and debris. The roof of the school was gone. The whole school, he feared, was gone.

Wind stung his face. The ceiling unzipped more, exposing more and more children to the falling debris. It wasn't just their own ceiling falling on them, it was stuff from outside too.

A final rending crash tore the rest of the ceiling away, and with that, a powerful gust of wind tore down the hallway. In a second—couldn't have been more—the hallway was a wind tunnel. Children came skittering down the linoleum floor, scattered by the wind like bowling pins. Two piled up against a fat woman, who had enough mass to keep her in place, and she stuck her leg out, trying to form a barrier to keep the children from flying past her. A child to Greg's right was spun away from the wall, and Greg thrust his own leg out to pin the child's ankle down to the ground.

In horror, he watched through eyes slitted against the rain of debris as a tiny form was whisked out of the hall and pulled into the air. The child disappeared over his head.

"Hold on!" he screamed to Holly, but the noise was lost in the shrill of the wind.

His punctured hand was hurting him, he was gripping her so hard, and he started to feel his grip with that hand weaken. No, no. Hold tight, hold tight, it had to be almost over. Bear the discomfort. It's nothing.

Something knocked him on the head, but he just closed his eyes and held tight to her. He felt the wind try to steal the child from under his leg. He clamped down harder.

Something big hit the shoulder of his injured hand.

At the same moment, Holly's legs lost their grip around his waist.

He felt the wind trying to steal her from him. He forced one eye open, and he could see her legs, pushed out away from him, in the air, parallel to the floor.

Hold on!

The wind was pushing the skin of her arm into ripples, like wind over a lake. In horror, he watched as the wind tore the uniform skirt from her body.

Impossibly, the wind seemed to grow harder, and his bad hand gave way entirely.

He had her by one arm.

The wind tore at her, tore and tore, and he almost lost her. She slipped. At the last second, he grabbed her arm, above the elbow, with his bad hand.

And the arm was still slipping through his good hand.

Holly. Stay with Daddy.

Damp with effort, and fear, and rain, his hand couldn't grip hard enough. He lost an inch. Then another. With a final whip, the wind tore his baby away.

Screaming back at the wind, he tried to move, to go after her, but it pushed him, and the child under his leg, along the tile and all the way to the base of the stairs and pinned them there.

The wind whistled. Something hit his back.

He had lost her.

He couldn't believe it. He had held on with all his might, and he had lost his only child, the only child he'd ever have, to the damnable wind.

The sound faded, and the wind with it.

He was able to open his eyes. He saw a tall boy, impaled on the end of the banister, as onto a spear. A crumpled adult body lay on the stairs. Screams sounded behind him.

But he could only look to the top of the stairs, stairs that disappeared into open air now, and the direction Holly had flown.

He disentangled himself from the boy he had saved and crawled on hands and knees up the first few steps. Pushing himself upright, he stumbled up the stairs, stepping over the adult's body, kicking away a brick, and a chunk of twisted metal, and then running up the last five steps and coming out onto a landscape of total destruction.

He turned, and there was the tornado, not very far away, still spinning, flinging out a sheet of steel, a sofa, a motorcycle, and hundreds upon hundreds of smaller, torn unidentifiable bits.

Holly.

Where was she? Let her not be one of those swirling bits. Let her be alive, please.

Dead or alive, either way, he had to find her.

Looking out over the scoured land that had once been a neighborhood, he didn't know where to start looking.

Captain T

It's devouring this town, shredding everything in its path. Doesn't matter if it's alive, or inanimate, wood or steal or brick or metal. Everything gives way to the force of this EF5 tornado.

And amazingly, we're seeing on our satellite other EF5s are touching down elsewhere. It's a swarm of them, an official outbreak. This day will go down in tornado history along with 2011 and 1974. And it'll be etched in the memory of this small town too.

I'm looking at a town map via satellite to see what else might have been there, in the path of destruction. We told you with the first tornado, the police station and city hall were hit—and the high school was just missed. It looks like an elementary school may have been in the path of the second one. And a history museum. Many neighborhoods. A Kmart. There's a train track too, east of town—we'll have to check about derailed train cars, as well, and make sure nothing dangerous has spilled out of any of them.

As you can see, I can't drive any farther on this road. And it seems a good place to park and get out, but I tell you, Captain-fans, I barely have the heart for it. I'm seeing what you're seeing via Felix's camera—hundreds of homes leveled. And I'm hearing what you might not be able to—people screaming, and children crying. There are people wandering like the lost, and bodies on the ground that we aren't filming, out of respect for the dead and their families. The smells of earth, of metal, of wood, of trash, of sewage. It smells bad.

And all this makes you appreciate how fragile life is. How many lives were lost today? What southern turn of the EF5 might not have killed me and Felix too? You're fine one moment, and the next moment?

Uploading and signing off while I see if I—if we—can help anyone here. People, appreciate the life you have right now. And love your roof and walls, even. You should be glad you have them.

Chapter 12

Sherryl was back in Jim's room at the care center. Down the hall, there had been panicked sounds as the second tornado went through town, but it had missed the home by a good distance. She hadn't even heard the wind.

She lay on her belly on his bed, her arm hanging over, stroking the bit of Jim she could feel. He hadn't said a word since she got back. She didn't think he was conscious.

"Ma'am?"

Glancing up, Sherryl saw a nurse's aide in a flowered uniform at the door, peering at her over the pile of fallen walls and ceiling.

"Are you okay?"

"I'm fine. Hardly a bruise."

"Is—?" The aide searched for the right way to ask it. "There's a patient in this room?"

"My husband." She shook her head. "There's nothing you can do for us."

"Oh. I'm sorry." She backed up, then hesitated, as if thinking about coming in.

"Don't worry, please," said Sherryl. "Help those who can be helped."

Without another word, the aide was gone.

Sheryl bent back to her vigil. She pressed her hand against Jim's chest and held her breath, waiting for the rise of it, or the fall, or the rattling feeling she had felt when he breathed a few minutes ago.

But there was nothing.

"Jim?" she said.

Nothing.

"Honey?" She closed her eyes and tried to feel with something other than her hand, some inner sense—was there any hint at all that he was still here? Or that he had gone?

There was nothing. She wanted something metaphysical or magical, but there was only the bare bed under her, and the smell of ruined wood and urine.

And poop, she realized. That was new.

Didn't they say people did that at the end? She'd never seen a death up close, so she didn't know if it were true or not. She'd had a cat once, a stray who'd adopted her, who she'd put down at the vet's, but the vet had politely covered the lower half of the cat with a towel when he had euthanized him.

"Jim?" she said, feeling more and more certain he was gone. The cat had had an easier time of it, she couldn't help but think. There was no movement under her hand at all. Just the pajama top, tacky with blood. "I hope I did the right thing. I hope you didn't hurt too badly."

She let go of his body and rolled onto her back, easing the strained muscle. She checked her watch. It was less than an hour after the first tornado had hit. If he had been in pain—and she couldn't lie to herself and say he had not been—at least it had been for less than an hour.

What had killed him? Did something crush his chest? Did he bleed to death? Damage his heart? Had he had a heart attack from fear?

She hoped fear hadn't killed him. Even more, she hoped that he had known she was with him.

She hoped most of all that she'd see him again one day in a better place.

Her hand was stained with blood. She wiped it on the mattress, but that didn't help much. It was already dry.

An urge to go into the bathroom and wash it off made her shake her head at herself. There wasn't going to be running water here.

It's time to go.

First, there was the work of digging her bag out from the pile of debris. She methodically pulled and pushed and wiggled it.

She saw her bag and Jim's foot at the same time.

Wasn't there a pulse you could feel for in the foot? She checked for one, but felt nothing. His skin felt cooler to her. That sign of death hurt her and reassured her in equal measure. He was gone—feeling no pain. He was really gone. And she was alone.

She found her bag half under the bed and pulled it out. Her car keys and cell phone were in her jacket pocket. Her bag was right here. She felt around under the bed to make sure nothing had fallen out of it, then checked inside the bag itself. Wallet, book, appointment book, sunglass case. If there was anything missing, it wasn't important.

She stood and dug her knuckles into her back, trying to ease the pain there, reaching as far around as she could reach. She was going to have to baby that—and if her house looked like this, she wasn't going to be able to. Picking up wreckage was going to be on the agenda for the next several days.

So. See if I can get Greg on the phone and make sure he's still okay. Drive to my house, if I can get there, and check it. Call the funeral home, or drop by, if either one is still standing, and make arrangements for Jim. Tell the receptionist here that there's a body, where it is, who it is, and have her tell that to whoever recovers bodies in this situation. Then go and help whoever needs help in town, starting with Greg, and then their—no, not their any longer, not with Jim gone—her neighbors, and any friend who asked. Then everyone else, help anyone who needed it.

Her organizing this list of things to do was a way not to think of Jim, she knew. But these *were* all things she did have to do. And she'd hold to them to avoid thinking too much of how Jim had passed and to avoid worrying if she'd done the right thing or not.

Even if she hadn't, it was impossible to change now.

She turned her back on the pile of rubble that had killed her husband, and she walked out of the room to start her final stage of life. A new stage.

I'm a widow now.

* * *

Greg spun in a slow circle, looking everywhere around the big empty lot that had been Central Elementary. The school was now a pit in the ground. Behind him was the basement corridor, open to the air. Over there, to the north, would be the larger pit that had been the cafeteria.

Except for those two holes, he had a hard time figuring out what was what. With houses scrubbed out of existence, and with debris scattered about, it was hard to even guess where the block ended. The prowl car was not where they had left it but a couple hundred yards to the east, on its tires, but looking as if it had been in a serious wreck.

Didn't matter. He wasn't driving anywhere. He was hunting for Holly.

"Holly!" he called.

If the car had gotten moved east, maybe she had too. Or maybe he should look south. She'd gotten pulled out of the hallway toward the south. He skirted the edge of the building's remains to the south, calling her name.

Every time he saw a big sheet of wood or drywall, he grabbed the corner and flipped it over, dreading what might be underneath. When he grabbed a piece of aluminum sheeting and sliced his palm, he remembered he still had the pink gloves.

He put them on and heaved the metal up, then over.

There was a small body underneath.

"No," he whispered. But then he saw it was a boy.

He wanted to leave him, but if someone else found Holly, hanging on to life, he wouldn't want them to do that. He'd want them to help. He knelt down among the broken bricks and wet papers and gingerly touched the boy. He was face up, and his face was cut up badly. Greg tried for a pulse and got nothing. Rested his hand on the chest and felt no movement. The boy was dead.

Holly.

He stood and called her name again. If the boy had come out of his basement corridor, she might be near. Greg mentally marked the piece of aluminum and plotted out a quarter circle, south and east of that. He'd walk in arcs, out from the boy's body.

"Officer!"

He looked over toward the voice. One of the parents or teachers was stumbling out of the open stairwell.

"I'm missing two students."

A teacher.

"There's a boy over here," he called back. "But he's—" Greg stopped himself as a child clambered up on hands and knees behind the teacher. He looked to the teacher and shook his head.

Her hands flew to her mouth.

Greg turned back to his own search.

"What should we do?" she called.

What *should* they do? "Be careful. Don't let any of the kids pick up something dangerous and get cut."

"But," she said, and trailed off as she took a good look around herself.

He couldn't spare time to comfort her or advise her. She was going to have to figure things out for herself while he searched for Holly. He went on, kicking aside lighter trash, working out from the boy's body. Each arc was more steps, back and forth, across his quarter-circle of land.

His radio crackled, but he ignored it. His gaze was fixed before his feet, hunting, looking for any sign at all.

A muddy scrap of material that might have once been white caught his eye. He bent down and picked it up, but it was a towel. Her shirt was white. Her skirt, plaid, was gone, probably a mile from here by now.

That reminded him of the tornado, and he looked out east. It was much farther away now. The damnable thing.

I'm going to find her.

He kept pacing his search area, back and forth.

Bending down, he pushed over a wooden futon, parallel slats that had somehow made it through their journey in the tornado.

And dropped to his knees when he saw a severed human arm.

He choked and spit bile to the side. Tenderly, he reached down but could see that it was too big to be Holly's.

It's someone's.

That person wasn't a somebody any longer.

He heard his name, and realized it wasn't the first time it had been shouted.

Reluctantly, he turned.

Massey. Vaguely, he realized it was good he had made it through okay.

Holly. The thought wouldn't leave his mind. She was the one fixed point in a mind twisted by fear and horror.

"Hey, what are you doing over there?" Massey yelled. "We have injured people."

"My daughter," he managed to say, before his throat closed up.

"Aww, shit," said Massey. "I—" He shook his head. "I have to help these people."

Greg nodded.

"I'll call the chief."

Greg turned back to his search. For long minutes he looked,

straining his shoulder once as he pushed aside a sofa, catching a piece of metal on his shin and cutting himself another time. He found another dead dog. No more bodies or body parts, thankfully.

"Holly!" he called out for the hundredth time.

He refused to think any thought but this: He'd find her. If he had to look for a week, he'd find her.

But it didn't take a week.

Chapter 13

The sun had come out, perversely, illuminating a scene of destruction that reminded Greg of old films he'd seen of Hiroshima. It was about to fall behind another squall line in the west when he saw her.

He didn't think it was her at first. The little dirty body lying on its side seemed too small.

But when he fell to his knees by it, he could see it was Holly. She had on the white uniform blouse, the pink flowered underwear, and the wispy brown hair.

The vision went blurry, and he realized that he was seeing her through tears. He dashed them aside and bent to her, afraid to touch her, terrified to know.

He touched her legs—so cold!—and took her hand to give it a soft squeeze.

"Daddy's here, sweetheart. I'm here."

He shouldn't move her, he knew, but her face was smashed up against the back of an easy chair lying on its side. He had to see her face.

Gently, trying to keep her spine as straight as possible, he rolled her onto her back.

Her forehead was covered with blood.

A mewl escaped him. "Holly, Holly, honey, wake up."

He pushed her hair away from the blood, and he saw a fresh welling of blood come out of a line in her forehead.

If it's welling, she's still alive.

Hope soared in his chest. He ripped off his uniform shirt and yanked off his T-shirt. Folding it, he pressed the cleanest side against the cut. With his left hand, he held it there while his right hand searched her muddy neck for a pulse.

His hand was shaking. He took a deep breath and willed himself to get control. For her sake, he had to snap to and let his first aid training take over.

Finally, he felt it—a weak pulse in her neck.

"Thank you," he said, to whoever might be listening out there. "Thank you for my baby's life."

Okay, he had risked enough damage by rolling her over. No more of that. He had to get her onto a back board.

He looked around himself. He had about a thousand items to choose from—plywood, chunks of fence, aluminum siding from metal buildings, an old-fashioned sled.

Digging around the debris, he found some heavy-duty electrical wire, and used it to lash his T-shirt to her forehead. Then he took up his uniform shirt and thrust his arms through the sleeves.

From his backboard choices, he selected a chunk of wood that had no nails sticking out of it, one not much bigger than Holly herself. He had to clear out a flat space next to her on the ground. He wished for a helper, but he knew Massey had his own hands full—and a wash of guilt came over him at the thought that he had left his partner alone to deal with the aftermath of the tornado.

Glancing around, he saw no one closer than a hundred feet— and most of them were combing through the debris too. Over at the school, a fire truck pulled up. Good. Medical care.

He eased Holly onto the backboard, then wrapped her on with

the rest of the wire, around the shoulders, then the waist, the hips and finally her knees. There was plenty of wire left over. He tried to break it, but it was impossible, so he wrapped it several times around the board and her ankles, until there was nothing left dangling for him to trip on.

He squatted alongside the stretcher and pushed his hands beneath it, at her shoulder and hips. Then he stood as smoothly as he could, lifting her.

It took forever to walk back to the school, trying not to stumble on the hundreds upon hundreds of bits of junk on the ground.

As he drew near, he saw several familiar faces—kids and teachers, the receptionist, and one of Holly's friends from the neighborhood, a boy named Jorge. Massey was working with a firefighter to haul people out of the pit in the ground that had once been the cafeteria.

Greg went to the fire truck, shouted, "Triage?"

"You have an injury?" A male EMT with a stethoscope around his neck climbed out of an open door and approached.

"My daughter." He could hear his voice break, feel his self-control hanging on by a thread. "Please."

"We'll take care of her." The EMT clapped him on the shoulder.

Greg eased her to the ground. "Will you take her to a hospital?"

The man held up a finger and began to examine Holly's still form. A distant part of Greg's mind knew what he was doing at most points—checking vital signs, looking for injuries hidden to the eye. The last thing, he cut through the wiring around her head and lifted off the blood-soaked T-shirt.

The EMT finally looked at Greg. "You did fine with first aid," he said. "I'm going to clean and bind the cut, and she'll go with the next load of kids."

Greg swallowed. "I want to stay with her."

"Until we go, sure you can," the man said. "But we'll want to transport the maximum possible, so no ride-alongs. You understand, right?"

Greg nodded. The logical part of him understood. The parent part wanted to curl himself around Holly to protect her and never let anyone take her out of his arms.

"You got her!"

Greg turned at the voice. Massey, carrying a limp boy in his arms. Massey waited while a firefighter walking just behind got a limping adult settled on the ground and covered with a reflective blanket, then Massey handed the firefighter the child, who stared vacantly into the distance, awake, but as responsive as a rag doll.

"Shock?" Greg said, of the boy.

"Maybe," said Massey. "No obvious injury. But how's your daughter?"

"Alive," said Greg.

"What happened to her?"

Greg told him.

"Wow, man. You're lucky she survived."

Greg didn't feel lucky as the EMT finished bandaging Holly and then tied a red triage tag around her arm. Red meant severe, transport first.

Massey said, "The chief wanted to talk to you."

Greg shook his head. He couldn't think of that right now.

"I'll try to get her on my radio," said Massey.

Greg watched the EMT check under Holly's back, feeling maybe for nails on the board or damage to Holly. He stood, feeling helpless. She was so still. So fragile and small and hurt.

He wanted to ask the EMT, Will she live? But he couldn't risk hearing the wrong answer. And the red triage tag told him enough. Not hopeless, because that'd be a black tag, but critically injured. And unconscious was never good.

The limping adult was being checked by the firefighter. He snapped a cold pack, handed it to the person and grabbed a green triage tag off the EMT's batch. The adult wasn't going to be helped any more than that—not anytime soon, not with that tag.

It finally registered with Greg that the adult was the principal of the school. His attention still half on Holly, he knelt down by the principal and said, "Are you okay?"

"Scratched up a bit, bounced around."

"Did you—" Greg cleared his throat. "Did you lose many on your side of the building?"

"A lot of injuries. Cuts, one open fracture they pulled out first, some smashed fingers and hands. How about your side?"

"We got at least three sucked out of the hall and outside into it." That's all he remembered, but there may have been more.

"God," she breathed.

"It was awful to see. Including my daughter, Holly Duncan."

"Of course, I know Holly. I'm so sorry. Is she—?"

Dead, he knew was the word she didn't want to say. "No. She's alive. But I found a boy who wasn't. And there was another one...." His mind flashed back to the impaled boy. "I wouldn't be surprised if there were a few more who didn't make it. The adults seemed to be too heavy for the wind to pull out. We tried our best."

She pulled an arm out from the blanket and gripped his forearm. "You did a good job."

He shook his head. Not good enough. Not even with his own child.

"You got back here in time. If we wouldn't have known in advance?" She let go of his arm and pointed to where the school had stood. "You and your partner saved dozens of lives by warning us. Including mine. Thank you."

Greg didn't want the thanks or the praise. He had failed to save everyone, and failed his own child. That was his job—his real job, not the job with the police. He was supposed to protect his child from harm, and he hadn't.

"I should have held on to her tighter," he said.

She grabbed his arm again and gave it a squeeze. "It's an act of God," she said. "I'm sure you did everything you could."

Massey said his name and Greg stood up, the principal's hand falling away as he did.

"What?" said Greg.

Massey wordlessly offered him his radio. Greg's was still attached to his slacks, but he had flipped it off while he was hunting for Holly and listening for her voice.

The realization that he might never hear that voice again stopped the words in his throat.

Massey pulled back the radio and spoke into it. "Hang on a second."

Greg drew a shaky breath and held his hand out, nodding an okay. He took Massey's radio. "Yeah? Over," he said.

"Duncan, Massey says you found your daughter. I'm glad to hear it. How are you?"

"Unhurt," he said.

"I mean, can you work? I know you must be upset, but we have less than 25 first responders on the ground, between police and Fire and even two retirees we've called in. Another day, I'd tell you to stay with your kid. They're mobilizing a National Guard Unit. But until they're here, I need you. Can you function?"

"I—wait, Chief. Let me think." He glanced at Massey as if the other man might have an answer. "Chief, I have to be with my child."

"I understand how you feel. But the town needs you too."

I'm going to quit this job anyway. He seriously thought about quitting it right now. But no—Holly was going to need insurance. Maybe rehab. Maybe—he shuddered at the thought—surgery. And he had gotten into police work to do some good, after all. Here's a last chance to do that. "Okay," he said, feeling a wrench of guilt. "I can't promise I'll be at my best, but I'll do what I can."

"Great—" the Chief said.

Whatever she was going to say next was lost in the thunderous sound of an explosion.

Everyone's head turned toward the sound. It came from about two blocks away.

A raging yellow fire was already alight, a swelling round bulb of it thrusting into the sky, pouring out black and gray smoke at its edges. As Greg watched, flaming debris rained out around the smoke cloud.

They all jumped as a chunk of metal hit not a hundred yards from the fire truck.

"Holy shit," said Massey.

In another second, all the firefighters around the school were running for the truck and yanking on fire gear.

Greg looked at the row of injured people from the school lying there. He grabbed the EMT. "You can't just leave these kids here."

"I'm staying right here," the EMT said. "I'll keep triaging until I'm told to go somewhere else."

"But—" Greg watched as the firefighters started gearing up to chase the fire. But what? Trade these lives for those at the fire?

He thumbed the radio on again. "Chief, we just had a major explosion here, two blocks or so west of here—maybe gas? Hang on." He called to a firefighter. "Was that a natural gas main?"

"That or a propane tank."

The smoke was drifting their way, and the uninjured evacuated from the school who were still standing around began to cough.

"Chief, yeah, it's a fuel fire. I think they're radioing to their chief now and I think they'll be sent to put that out. Over."

"You and Massey need to stay with the school. There are still injured there, right?"

Greg handed the radio over to Massey, who had heard the question.

"This is Massey. We still have about ten casualties in the cafeteria, a couple pretty bad, and a lady who's too heavy to lift out. We'll need equipment of some sort to get her up."

"Get the rest of them but her out. I'll coordinate with Fire and tell you what to do after I check with the fire chief."

To Greg, watching the firefighters gear up to go, the city seemed too disorganized. Wasn't there a list of priorities somewhere? But then he realized there were no perfect answers to any of this. Twenty-five first responders. Probably dozens dead, and probably a hundred needing fast medical care. Hundreds of people who needed lesser assistance, who were having to wait for it. Another group of first responders was stuck in the collapsed police station, wanting to get out. It was like some horrible puzzle. He was glad it wasn't his to work out.

He mentally shook himself, trying to separate the professional side of him from the father side. If he could grow wings and fly, he'd pick Holly up and fly her to a hospital. If his car was a block away and working, he'd drive her there. But for now he'd let the EMT care for her and he'd do his own part for other people's children.

The firemen helped move the injured away from the truck, and then they leapt onboard and, with a beep of their siren, pulled out, heading for the fire. They had to honk to get people out of their way. Greg looked down the street and saw dozens of people looking through debris of homes, and some wandering, looking dazed and lost. A few seemed to be parents, hurrying toward the school.

He glanced down at himself and saw the uniform. They wouldn't give a crap about him having an injured child. He was an official, and they'd expect something from him.

Quickly, he bent and planted a kiss on Holly's cheek. He tapped the EMT on the shoulder where he was working on the boy. "Tell me the truth. How serious is she?"

"There's no obvious skull fracture. But there's no way to know what's going on in her brain that's keeping her unconscious. For now she's stable. I'll keep a close eye on her."

"With your guys at the fire, I need to help rescue the rest of the kids." He pointed at the ruins of the north side of the school.

"I'll give you a high sign if anything changes with your kid."

"Thank you."

He flipped on his radio again and strode over to Massey, who had put his radio away.

"I hate leaving Holly," Greg said to him as they started back to the school, "but I'm coming to help you."

He only looked back at Holly once on the walk over. He felt physically pulled in both directions.

"Pay attention to what you're doing down here," Massey said, as they approached the pit where the cafeteria had been. "You won't do her any good if you get yourself hurt too."

The one thing you could say for the tornado. The winds had been so powerful that when the school had blasted apart, much of the brick and steel had been blown east of the basement. If it had all fallen straight down onto them, there would have been many more injuries.

Not that there wasn't plenty of junk strewn around in the pit. He couldn't begin to inventory it all—a turquoise electric guitar, PVC pipes, crumbled plaster, a School Zone traffic sign on a concrete base, branches, a window frame, a whole bathroom vanity from someone else's home with its doors ripped off, and a big pile of Cheerios that had escaped their bag but were still in a neat pile.

How could Holly, a fifty-pound child, be ripped out of his grip while Cheerios just sat there? It wasn't fair.

Mostly, the debris was wood—all over the ground, in the pit that had been the cafeteria, the lumber from hundreds of destroyed homes was strewn everywhere.

"You steady the ladder, and I'll go down," said Massey.

It was only then Greg saw that the top of the staircase was

gone. A metal ladder from the fire truck was extended down to the first solid step.

"You've been hauling people up that?"

"The kids are pretty easy, if they don't fight you," Massey said.

Greg looked at him with new respect. Not a job for anyone with a fear of heights.

The male teacher he'd spoken to after the first tornado was down there, apparently unhurt, but missing his shirt. He seemed to be keeping everything under control.

"Rick!" Massey called, and the teacher looked up. He hurried over to the stairway and braced the ladder.

Massey swung his leg around the ladder. "He'll steady it for the first few steps," he said to Greg. "Wait until I'm down, and he'll do the same for you."

Massey went down the ladder and slipped past the teacher, who called up, "Ready if you are."

Greg tested the ladder, pushing it to either side to see how easily it slipped. It was not an ideal situation, but there was nothing else to do. He swung his leg over and went down as quickly as he could.

At the end, Rick said, "Wait a second," and then moved and said, "Okay. You're clear."

"Thanks."

"We have only two more seriously injured. I got the bleeding stopped on Lupe's leg, so she can wait until the second load."

"Show me the way to the worst one."

He was led to a little girl who held her hands up in the air. Dried tears had left tracks on her cheeks.

Rick said, "Her hands are pretty smashed up."

Greg tenderly took her arm at the elbow to steady it and looked closely at the damage on one hand. Something heavy—a table or piece of furniture—had smashed her hand good. There was blood oozing out around her fingernails, and her whole hand was purple. Her skin felt tacky.

How was he going to carry her if she couldn't hold on? And how was he going to get her up there without bouncing her hands against something?

But looking more closely at her face, he thought he had to get her up fast. She was terribly pale, and looked like she might be in shock, which could be fatal to anyone, but kids could crash fast.

But how do I get her up the ladder?

He got her to lie on her back, settled her hands across her belly—she made a sound when he did—and cradled the child in his arms. She weighed little, and he rose easily to his feet. She was lighter than Holly. "Follow me to the ladder, please," he said to Rick. He needed all the help he could get with the ladder's stability.

Could he back up it? No, no way. Shifting his grip on the child, he got her balanced so that one of his own hands could grip the ladder's side rail. He kept feeling as if he were going to fall to the other side, and hurt them both, but he managed to stay balanced. Had the child been fidgeting or fighting him, though, it would have been impossible.

At the top, he had to set her onto the ground to finish getting himself safely up. Then he bent and took her up again and hurried her over to the EMT's triage station.

They needed more equipment. He hoped people from nearby fire and police departments were rushing toward town even now.

He watched the EMT for a half a minute as he checked the girl. "Find me something like a big brick, or a plastic box, would you?" he asked Greg. "To elevate her feet."

Greg scanned the ground and saw something that might work. He went to the square of dirty gray plastic and saw it was someone's fishing tackle box. He brought it back.

"Good, thanks."

Greg wanted to ask about Holly, but the man was busy, so he checked on her by himself. She was lying still on her board, with a Mylar blanket over her now. He couldn't stop himself from checking the pulse at her neck, which he knew wasn't going to tell him anything. Realizing there was nothing to identify her, he fished out his wallet and found an official Police Department business card with his name on it. He tucked it into her shirt pocket. He planted a kiss on a dirty cheek and went back to the school to finish carrying the rest of the injured children out.

As he walked back to the cafeteria pit, he noticed a new line of thunderstorms ahead—but it was five or six miles north of them. A small blessing.

After his third trip up, a child clinging to his chest like a chimp, a woman ran over to him, crying the child's name. It might have been a stranger, or a kidnapper, and under other circumstances he would have asked for ID, but when the child reached for the woman, he handed it over. He started guiding them toward the triage station in the failing afternoon light, and he realized that Holly was gone. They'd taken her away to a hospital.

Only then did he realize he had no idea which one.

* * *

Sherryl's drive home took her past the south side of the first tornado's trail. To the north, homes and businesses had been razed, their structures and contents spewed out everywhere. Thinking of everything those people had lost distracted her from her own grief.

She arrived home to find her own house standing, and felt a wave of relief that made her feel light enough to drift off the ground. Then guilt came, smashing her mood back down. How could she have a home, still, when so many others did not?

Her garden had taken some damage from winds. The crocuses were beaten down into papery wads. Random pieces of paper skittered along her lawn, driven by a pleasant breeze. To the west, the sun shone orange. She got her cell phone out and checked the time. It was 5:30. The sun would set in 45 minutes. And then whatever cleanup efforts were underway would be made a hundred times harder.

She tried phoning Greg but got no signal. Unlocking the door to her house, she set down her bag and went to the landline. She tried Greg, then her closest friends. She got a recording or a strange whining tone until she tried, as a last measure, her church. The line was busy, so she walked into the living room with the phone and hit redial. She checked the television, but there was no power. She'd forgotten to turn on her car radio—that'd have to be her source of news. The fourth time she dialed the church, the line rang.

A harried female voice answered on the fifth ring.

She gave her name. "I attend there. I'm wondering what to do to help."

"Our church is still standing, so we're setting up emergency housing for displaced families here. We need cots, bed linens, futons, sleeping bags, air mattresses, toothbrushes, clean towels and washcloths, food, anything you can donate."

"Do you need volunteer staff?"

"No, I think we're okay there, but I appreciate you asking. I'm sorry, another line is ringing. Thank you!" And she was gone.

So what I'll do, Sherryl thought, is gather things for the church, and then I'll go to Greg's, and one by one check out my friends in person. If none of them need help, I'll randomly help whoever is in need. It'll be dark soon, so I need flashlight, lantern. Work gloves. Heavier jacket.

She realized, with a stab of pain, that Jim wouldn't need his clothes any more. She still had a closet full here. Okay, they'd go to a good cause. She'd gather shirts, jackets, shoes, hand over a bagful to the church and leave the rest in her trunk. No doubt she'd run across someone who could use a jacket tonight.

By the time she had her car packed, the sun had almost set. Streetlights were out, so she drove cautiously to the church and dropped off her donations. It took three trips from the car. The receptionist handed her a receipt—letterhead with "Donations" scrawled on it. "Fill it in yourself," she said.

Sherryl drove up Central until the tornado damage stopped her. She parked and grabbed one of Jim's jackets from the trunk, and threw it on over her own. Her gloves on, a flashlight in hand, and she was ready to try and help.

A bright light drew her forward. Spotlights were set up at the center of town. She could see a big fire truck, a backhoe, and a pair of generators. Police tape kept a small crowd back.

Until then, she hadn't known the courthouse was damaged. Only the foundation and two or three courses of bricks had survived, except for one wall where bricks remained to about shoulder height. The police station was nothing but a grid of metal, and a few of the beams were twisted into freakish shapes.

She asked another person looking on, a man who looked familiar but whose name she couldn't remember. "What's happening?"

"They just rescued the police from the basement. Now they're trying to find the mayor and city clerk and so on from city hall. But it doesn't look good, does it?"

Sherryl stared at the scattering of brick and stone around the historic city hall. No, it didn't look good at all. "How many in the police building?" Had Greg been there? "Are they all okay?"

"Nothing but minor injuries."

She began scanning the crowd.

"Missing someone?" the man asked.

"My nephew is on the police force."

"I might know him. What's his name?"

"Greg Duncan."

He shook his head. "What's he look like? Plainclothes or uniform?"

"Uniform. He's 32, just under six feet, good-looking kid, very short dark hair."

"White guy?"

"Yes, he is."

She scanned the crowd and tried to figure out what was going on. There were a group of people with blankets around their shoulders—rescued people—and Greg wasn't among them. A couple of guys in reflective vests were directing the backhoe at the courthouse. Other people were concentrating on different buildings in the square, looking for survivors or bodies.

"Did you hear about the fire up on Hawthorne?" the man asked.

"No. I've been with my husband at the care facility—you know the nursing home by the high school?" she said. "I just came out here a few minutes ago, trying to figure out how I can help."

"So the nursing home came through okay?"

"No," she said. "It was pretty badly hit."

The man opened his mouth, possibly to ask about her husband, thought better of it, and turned again to watch the rescue operation.

She saw one of the people toss off the blanket and turn to walk out of the light. It was a woman, dust covering her hair. She grabbed a guy by the shirt and spun him around, apparently not pleased with him.

Sherryl recognized him then—it was Greg.

She slipped under the yellow tape and walked toward him, finally recognizing the woman as the new police chief. "Greg," yelled Sherryl.

They both looked over and Greg pulled away from the woman and came trotting over. Sherryl opened her arms and he came into them, holding on to her. He was muddy. His hand and arm were bandaged.

"I'm so glad you're okay," she said, feeling tears threatening.

"Holly," he said, his voice breaking.

Oh, no. She pushed back to look at him.

"She's hurt bad, and I can't get to her."

"Where is she?"

"I can't even find that out. A hospital down in Cincinnati is all I know."

"We'll figure it out."

"How? There aren't any phones and the cells—"

"We'll drive down there. My cell phone will start working at some point, as soon as we hit a tower."

"Your car is okay?"

"Miraculously, yes. The tornado just missed it."

"I just saw mine. It looks like it's been through the crusher at the junk yard."

"And my house is standing."

"I doubt mine is. Central Elementary was leveled by the second tornado, and my house was in its path."

"That doesn't matter. You know you can stay with me."

"Will you take me down? Now to Cinci?"

She looked over his shoulder. Someone else was talking with the chief. "Do you need to tell your chief you're headed out?"

"If I do, she might fire me on the spot. And I can't afford to lose insurance with Holly in the hospital."

"You have to tell her that you're going, don't you?"

"I'll radio her in a minute. Let's get going while we can."

She pointed in the direction her car was parked. Once there, she opened the trunk and pulled out a bag of Jim's clothes.

She got in the car and tossed the bag at Greg. "Find something clean to put on."

"These are Jim's?"

"He's dead, Greg."

"Oh, Sherryl. I'm so sorry."

"I keep telling myself it's a blessing."

"It can't feel that way, though."

She shook her head and started the car. "Let's get going. Unless you want to stop by my house and clean up? Shower probably works, but the electricity is out."

"No. I want to find my daughter."

She took them south on Central, which turned into a two-lane highway for a few miles. "Don't forget to call your boss," she said.

"Thanks. I had forgotten." He took out his radio and got the chief on it. The exchange was brusque. He finished by saying, "I'll be back, I promise. I just need to find her, and I won't stay long. I'll be back here before nine tonight, at the latest." He glanced at Sherryl, who nodded her agreement. She could get him back by then.

When he got off he pulled out his cell phone. "Damn," he said. "Battery's dead."

She said, "My smartphone is in my bag. Take it out and as soon as there's a signal, start hunting for hospitals online."

She sped south along the dark highway.

Chapter 14

"We need her insurance information."

Malika knew better than to volunteer that her family was on MyCare, Ohio's Medicaid. She wanted treatment as good as any rich person would get—at least until they found her out as a poor person. So she did what she seldom did, and she lied. "I don't know."

"It's fine, don't worry," said the ambulance attendant, a dark-haired white woman. "I have to go, but they'll take good care of you."

"Thank you for bringing me." She had been transferred out of the fire truck just south of Fidelity and hadn't had a chance to thank the firefighters who had rescued her.

"Take care," the woman said, and left her in the care of a male nurse, who was still writing down what the ambulance woman had been telling her.

"Okay, let's look at your legs," he said, finishing his notes. His eyebrows were raised as he lowered the sheet back over her.

That didn't seem good.

"I'm going to get you into X-ray," the nurse said.

It happened fast enough that Malika really did start to worry. The last time she'd been in an ER had been with Antoine, and that had taken hours and hours. She must really be in trouble if they were moving this quickly.

In the X-ray lab, they took two shots of both her legs. "We need to turn you on your side," the attendant said. "I'm afraid it might hurt."

"I'm doped up," said Malika. She felt the pain, but distantly, as if it were a tinny, broken-up sensation felt through a cell phone, if a person could feel things through a cell phone. Maybe they'd invent that. That, or the smell phone. Smell phone? She must be pretty high.

The attendant had Malika grab on to the edge of her bed, hold her breath, and took more pictures from that direction. "You may need an MRI before you're done," she said. "Ever had one of those?"

"No, ma'am," Malika said.

"It's noisy, but it doesn't hurt a bit," she said. "You claustrophobic?"

"Not at all." Though she never wanted to be pinned by a fallen building again.

"That's good." She pushed Malika out into the hallway and said, "Someone will be here in a second to take you back."

Malika's mind drifted for a while, and then she was on the move again, back to the ER, where a short Indian doctor with a lilting accent examined her.

"What did you do to yourself?" he said.

"I got fell on," Malika said, and felt her face flush at the bad grammar. "A tornado. The ceiling fell," she said.

"Ah. One of the tornado traumas. I suspect we'll be seeing more," he said, and leaned over to tap something into a computer keyboard. "A specialist will be here in a few minutes. Do you need something for pain?"

"I'm still high from the last shot."

"Don't hesitate to ask for more. Any allergies?"

She shook her head.

"What did she have?" The nurse mumbled something. "Morphine, p.r.n," he said to the male nurse, writing something down, and then he was gone without a goodbye.

The nurse stuck a needle into her arm, and someone else came and took blood.

Malika felt as if she were on some bizarre tour of the hospital as she was moved yet again, pushed along long hallways, watching fluorescent lighting sweep by overhead, getting taken into an elevator. When she looked over, she realized the person in the elevator with her, pushing her, was someone new, a black man.

"Where are we going?" she asked the stranger.

"Critical care."

"I don't feel critical."

"They're just being careful," he said.

Upstairs, she saw two more doctors in quick succession. The first one had her X-rays and examined her legs. "You're lucky," he said. "It looks like there's micro fracture in your right tibia, but it shouldn't need to be set."

"I think it's starting to hurt again," she said. "Comes and goes."

He leaned close to her. "Tell me about it. Describe the pain to me."

She tried to concentrate through the drug's fading fuzziness. "At first, it was like fire."

"When you got pinned?"

"No. I couldn't feel a thing for a while, then. When they got the roof or whatever off me."

"Go on."

She tried to tell him how it had felt then, and how it was different now—less burn-y and more of a throb. He nodded, looking sympathetic. It was easy to talk to him. But talking about the pain seemed to make it hurt more again.

"It's gotten worse since we've been talking?" he said.

She nodded. "Are you going to have to cut my legs off?"

"No, no," he said, and he patted her arm. "We might do some minor surgery. The damage is to the muscles, maybe to a nerve."

"Will I walk again?"

"It might take a few weeks, and it'll hurt at first, but you should be able to walk."

"Thank you, Jesus," she said.

"I'll order you some more pain medication, once we check the time on your last."

She couldn't help him on that. She had lost all track of time. Where was Adam? Maybe he was here, but trailing her route through the hospital would be like going on a scavenger hunt.

"My mother and a friend should be coming."

"We'll get your mom here, don't worry."

He left and was replaced by another doctor, a Chinese woman with a blunt haircut and big round glasses. "I'm the renal specialist," she said.

"Renal—that's...." Malika knew what it was, but her mind wasn't working very well.

"Kidneys."

"Are my kidneys hurt? I haven't needed to pee since I got here."

"It's complicated, but it has to do with compounds your muscles release in an accident like this. I just wanted to introduce myself in case we have to put you on dialysis in the next couple days."

"Dialysis?" She knew what that was, but the doctor misunderstood and explained anyway.

"We might have to filter your blood through a machine if your kidneys get overwhelmed with the chemicals your body is producing right now. If it happens, it won't go on for long. Just until the bad chemicals get cleared out of your system."

"And I'm making chemicals because of something falling on my legs?"

"Yes."

"So nothing hurt my kidneys, like the wall falling or whatever?"

"No, they're uninjured. It's purely a chemical reaction."

"That's interesting."

The smile came and went so quickly, Malika wasn't sure she'd seen it. "It is, actually."

"When will you know?"

"We're going to test your blood—a lot, every hour today—and we'll know from that."

"What are you testing for?"

The doctor studied her. "Potassium, phosphate, myoglobin, creatine," she said.

"I'll look those up."

"You have a smartphone with you?"

"Oh no, I don't even own a cell phone. I meant, I will when I can get to a computer."

"Okay," she said and stood up. She didn't pat Malika's arm, which made her the first one. "I'll see you soon—even if it's just to tell you everything is okay."

"Wait. Do you know are there many people from my town here? Getting treated?" She couldn't be the only one injured.

"I don't know, I'm sorry. Bye, now," the doctor said and went away.

For the first time, Malika realized her whole family could be hurt—or dead. Or Adam's mom could be. The people in her church, her minister, her teachers. Her debate team. Or anyone at all. She began to worry about each person she knew and cared for.

She didn't have to worry for long. Another nurse came and added something to her IV, and Malika drifted off into a fuzzier, pain-free world, and then to sleep.

* * *

When Sherryl's cell phone approached a working tower, it began to beep at Greg. She had texts and phone messages, more than 25 of them. He told her and offered the phone back.

She shook her head. "Nothing's as important as finding Holly."

As he hunted for hospital numbers, Sherryl drove off the two-lane section of highway and onto a newer four-lane stretch, leading into Cinci. It was better lit, with orange sodium lights every hundred feet. She sped up. "Tell me when you know where I'm going."

"I'm trying to call them in order, starting with the northwestern most."

It was the third one he tried. "Do you have a child, Holly or NFN Duncan?"

"I'm not able to give out any patient information over the phone."

"I'm her father, a Fidelity police officer. I left my business card in her clothing. Can you check, please?"

He was put on hold and a few minutes later the hospital operator came back on the line. "Describe the card to me."

"Fidelity PD, badge on the left, my name, 'Police Officer' under that, fax, phone, website."

"Yes, sir. We have her here."

"Thank God," he said. "I'm on my way." He clicked off and looked up the hospital and got a route to it. The minutes dragged while Sherryl drove to it.

Sherryl let him out in front of the hospital, and he ran inside. He had to stop at a metal detector and show the guard his gun and badge. There was a receptionist at the front wearing a "volunteer" badge. A lot of people were milling around the desk. Greg pulled his badge out of his pocket again, grateful he had it. It was a magical key that could open doors more quickly.

Her looking up the name seemed to take forever. "I have a Greg Duncan listed, in PICU. Third floor."

"That's me—her," he said. "Tell my aunt, please. Sherryl Higgins. She's parking her car. Let her know where I've gone."

He was three steps away when he realized he didn't know where he was going. "Elevators?" he called back. The volunteer was on the phone, and she pointed to a wall then motioned to go back.

Greg sped through the hall until he saw the elevator sign and punched the button. After a few seconds, he punched it again, knowing it for the stupidity it was. Keeping his eye on the hall, thinking Sherryl might get here before the elevator, he bounced on his toes, nervous.

No, not nervous. Terrified, to be honest.

With a quiet *bing*, the elevator doors opened and a man with a walker got out. Greg held the door for him and the man nodded his thanks. The doors seemed to hang open forever as he punched the button for the third floor.

It opened on the second floor to let in a hospital worker. When it opened on the third, he hurried out and began scanning the hallways, looking for signs, arrows, a directory, seeing none of that. He pushed through a set of double doors and found a nurse at a station, typing into a computer.

"Excuse me," he said. "Where is PICU?"

"Oh, it's in the other wing. Sort of hard to get to. You might want to take the elevator back down and take the other bank up."

"Can I get there from here, on this floor?"

"It's complicated," she said.

"Maybe you could draw me a map?" He wanted to reach across and shake her, or force her to take him there. But he controlled himself. He was close, now at least, after the awful forty minutes of trying to hunt Holly's location from the car.

I keep losing her.

It was irrational, he knew, but since the wind had torn her out of his arms, it felt like something was trying to take her away from him—with the ambulance taking her away while his back was turned, and depositing her who-knew-where, and now even this.

"Please," he said. "It's my daughter."

She pulled over a pad of paper and drew him a map. Then she explained it to him. Don't turn at that sign, but at this. If you're seeing offices, you've gone wrong. If you're in a covered walkway, you've gone too far.

He controlled his impatience until she was done explaining, and then he grabbed the map and took off down the hallways, trying to follow her scrawls and decipher the medical abbreviations. He got turned around once, but he found an orderly to set him straight.

The seconds ticked away, making him crazy with worry. He should have never let Holly out of his sight in the first place. When the wind grabbed at her, he shouldn't have ever let her go. It was his fault she was hurt.

By the time he got to the PICU, he was panting. No one was at the main nurse's station. He had to wait. A distant elevator dinged, and before a nurse appeared, his aunt did.

She came up to him and threaded her arm around his waist. "Calm down if you can, Greg. You look like you're about to have a stroke."

"I might be."

A nurse came through swinging doors, pushing a trolley. He said, "Holly Duncan. I'm Greg Duncan, her father."

"You said they had her down as Greg," his aunt said.

"Right. There was a business card with her, with my name on it."

"Can I see some ID?" the nurse asked.

Greg pulled out his wallet for his driver's license and showed her his badge. The woman said, "Do you have an insurance card?"

"Yes," he said, digging that out of his wallet.

"Just a second, and I'll ring for someone to take you in."

"Just tell me where she is."

"Let me call a doctor first."

God, that had to mean bad news. "Is she—?" He couldn't make himself say the word "dead."

The nurse seemed to understand and shook her head. "She's resting. You'll want someone to answer questions."

"She's okay?"

"We're taking good care of her, Officer. Just give me a second." She turned her back and picked up a phone, calling someone and speaking in a voice too low to hear.

"I have my phone," said Sherryl. "You'll want to call Holly's mother."

He had forgotten all about her. "I will when I know what to tell her," he said.

The swinging doors opened again, and a short pale-skinned man in white stood there. "Mr. Duncan?"

"I'll wait here," said Sherryl.

Greg stepped forward with equal parts eagerness to have his eyes on Holly again and trepidation. "Is she okay?"

"She's still unconscious," the man said. "I'm Dr. Arons, a neurologist specializing in peds." He led Greg through a hall with rooms that had glass windows, so that the patients were all visible from the hall. He passed a baby in a crib with two parents, a child alone, hooked up to machines, a pre-teen sitting up in bed, reading a comic book while a woman sat next to him knitting.

The doctor turned into the next room and Greg took a deep breath, trying to prepare himself for whatever.

Holly was lying on a hospital bed, looking tiny in comparison to the bed, on a ventilator. An IV went in her hand. She was hooked up with leads to one large machine, and with others to a portable machine on a wheeled cart.

Greg said, "Can I touch her?"

"Of course."

He stepped to the bedside and bent over her, whispering in her ear. "Daddy's here, sweetie. I'm right here. Everything's going to be all right." He hoped it was so. He found a spot on her head where no wires were attached and gave her a soft kiss.

"You cleaned her up," he said.

"Yes. So she was in the tornado, I hear."

Greg told him, haltingly, of the moments in the basement, the roof getting ripped off, the wind lifting her, losing his grip. He could feel it, in his palm, the feeling of her skin being pulled along, losing her. By the time he was done with the story, tears were pooled in his eyes and he couldn't see for them. "I should have held on tighter. My damned hand wouldn't hold." He held up his bandaged hand.

"Don't blame yourself," the doctor said. "Sounds like if you would have let go sooner, she might not have made it."

"Will she make it?" Greg asked, afraid to hear the answer.

"Her vital signs are stable. She has some bruises, a few minor cuts, but apart from her head injury, she's fine. She's not seizing. X-rays show a hairline fracture right here—" and he reached over and touched Holly's head two inches over the left temple —" but it's not in itself the cause for worry."

"What is?"

"That she hasn't been conscious in—what? How many hours?"

Greg checked his watch. "Three—just over three hours."

"She's going to get MRIed within the hour. I want to look at the brain."

"What—" Greg coughed to clear his throat. "What are you looking for?"

"Swelling, bleeding. See if there's any situation that we can treat."

"You mean brain surgery?" Greg gripped the railing of the bed.

"Without knowing, I can't predict what we'll want to do. Perhaps drugs, perhaps minor surgery. Perhaps keep her in an induced coma. Could be one of a number of interventions are indicated. Or," he said, switching his gaze to Holly, "we might have to simply wait."

"For?"

"For her to wake up, to get better, or to get worse." The doctor shrugged one shoulder. "I wish I could tell you with more certainty, but we're very much in a wait-and-see mode until we get that MRI. What I can tell you is that her Glasgow score is not terrible."

"That's what?"

"A scale that tells us how responsive she is. If you don't mind, I'll show you."

"Yes. Please."

"I'm going to pinch her, to hurt her a little."

He reached over and took a fold of skin on Holly's still hand, the one without the IV, and gave it a sharp pinch. She drew away, made a sound, and her eyelids fluttered. "You see?"

"I don't know what I'm seeing."

"She's responsive to pain, but not to our voices. If you don't mind trying, say something."

Greg leaned over her and said, "Holly, honey, wake up. It's Daddy."

"Louder."

"Holly, wake up!" She didn't. He turned to the doctor. "That's bad?"

"There was a little twitch of her facial muscles. It could mean something. Her pupils are equal-sized too, and respond to light. That's all good."

"But she's not waking up."

"That's of concern."

"What can I do? Should I keep talking to her?"

Slowly, the doctor shook his head. "It wouldn't hurt, but I can't promise it'll help. I wish I could give you something more concrete to do. I know this is hard for you. But there's nothing *to* do. For now just wait."

"I have to get back to work tonight." He hated it. But he had promised.

"Is your wife...?"

"We're divorced. She lives in Atlanta. I have custody. I have an aunt here—the only other family in town. Will you let her sit with Holly when I'm not here?"

"I'll fix it so she can."

"Thank you." Greg wanted to stay. But how much good could he do here? He hated this. Hated feeling so helpless. Hated looking down at Holly and seeing her hooked up to those machines, unmoving. Hated his obligation to the job. Hated the damned tornado most of all.

"I'll let you be alone with her while I check on getting her that MRI," the doctor said.

A half-hour later they came to get Holly to take her for the scan. The person outside the double doors, not the one who had been there before, but a person in street clothes, called him over and gave him back his insurance card.

"They said they'd okay you to go inside," he said to his aunt. "Can I impose on you—?"

"Oh Greg, you know it's not an imposition."

"She looks so helpless," Greg said.

She took his hand, squeezed it, and let it drop. "I'll stay as long as you need me to. All night, I assume. I hope you don't mind, but I've taken the liberty of doing a few things."

"What?"

"I filled out some forms for you. And I called your mother."

"Oh, right. Of course. Thank you."

"She didn't answer, but I left a message."

"I appreciate it."

"And I called a car rental agency. They're delivering a car here for you. If yours isn't drivable, you'll need one."

"I'll need to drop by and get a cell phone charger."

"You can use mine to call your ex."

He reached out his hand, but when he had the phone, he realized he didn't know her number. "I need my phone to get her number," he said to his aunt with a shrug. "I guess it'll have to wait until I buy a charger. Maybe by then I'll know more."

"You don't have it written down anywhere?"

"At home. But I doubt we have a home any more. And it was on her school records, but the paper version is blown halfway to Dayton by now." He said, "I realize I haven't noticed any computers in the debris. Isn't that strange? Everybody had one. The school probably had dozens."

"You probably did see some, in pieces."

"Maybe. Come to think of it, I've seen three dead dogs, several injured ones, some muddy ones crawling out of collapsed buildings, and no cats."

"Pretty clever at hiding, cats."

"Why am I talking about cats? I have a daughter who's unconscious, a job that's hanging on by a string, a house that's no doubt gone, and my uncle just died."

"For all that, you seem to be doing pretty well."

"Thanks to you. I'm so sorry about Jim. Do you want to talk about it?"

She waved it off. "Later." Her phone rang, and she answered. "Yes. Thank you." She hung up. "The car's here. You go down, show your license, insurance card, take the guy back to his office, and it's yours for a week at a time."

"Let's go over to the desk," he said. He introduced her to the woman there and explained that he wanted all medical information released to her. Was there anything he had to sign?

The woman's eyebrows lifted in judgment as she realized he was leaving.

"I don't want to go," he told her. "But I'm a police officer. My town is in ruins. If she wakes up, if there's any change at all, I can be back in an hour."

"I'll let the doctor know."

There was a form to sign—several, in fact. He got that done, and was about to leave when Sherryl called him over.

"Here's my house key. Use it if you need it. Lock it and leave it under the mat."

"That's not secure."

"Quit being such a cop. I know that. I wouldn't normally, but this is a special situation."

Greg hugged her, then went down to pick up his rental car. It took him another half-hour to take the fellow back to his office, but he glimpsed the sign he wanted to see on the way. Thank God for Walmarts. With any luck, he'd be able to grab the right phone charger.

That's when he realized that they couldn't call him if Holly needed him, not until the cell system was back up in town. He nearly turned around and went back to the hospital.

But no. He had promised to go back to work. Other people needed help. His boss was right—he had a commitment to them too. And if Holly just lay there, unconscious, he'd drive himself crazy watching her.

With any luck, they'd get something rigged up to replace the downed towers within a day. Still, guilt was his passenger as he drove north, out of cell range, and into the damaged town he had sworn to serve and protect.

On the way, he listened to the radio news. There were dozens of tornados all over Indiana and southern Ohio, and now those same cells were moving into Pennsylvania, spinning out more twisters. Their second one might be one of the biggest, but their town was not the largest that had been destroyed. Dayton had been hit by the same one—and there, its path was a full mile wide. Greg was pretty sure he had been looking at less than half that. He tried to remember the scene at the school—at least three blocks to the north had looked to be razed, and two to the south.

When he got within range, Greg radioed in to Rosemary. The dispatcher told him to come in to the police station.

He got stopped on the highway by a familiar-looking man with a Maglite. When Greg placed his badge at the window, he got waved through.

Downtown, he parked his car as near as he could get to the center of town and walked in to find Rosemary swamped. "We need crowd control," she said. "Until we get more lights, at least. We have as many rescuers as we can use for the generators and lights we have. As soon as we get more set up, I'll pull you in to those so you can do search and rescue."

"Why crowd control? Are there riots?"

"No. We have media, we have first responders from other locations coming in, we have people who say they're relatives but are probably looters. We're trying to limit access on the main highways. We're having road crews put up barriers at the minor roads, hoping it'll deter the casual snoops."

"Okay, so what do you need me to do?"

"I want you to take over on south Central. We have a roadblock up. And Jay Jackson—do you know him, retired a few years back?"

"Yeah, I know him."

"He's manning it alone right now. I want someone official there."

Greg looked down at himself. "I won't look any more official than him. My uniform shirt was filthy, and bloody. I'm in civies now as you can see."

"Can't you get a shirt from home?"

"I don't think I have a home."

"Damn. Just take one of the yellow vests, over there."

Before that night, Greg had not guessed what this sort of duty would be like. He supposed every fire and police officer had thought about disaster work. It's the post 9/11 world, so you can't help but imagine yourself there, or at the Boston bombing, or at Katrina, wondering how you'd hold up.

But this manning the barricade—this duty was just bizarre.

There was media, including one big satellite van with call letters he knew, coming up from Cincinnati. He directed them to the center of town, where Rosemary and any other officials could deal with them.

There were people with SUVs full of bottled water, blankets, simply wanting to help. He knew they might be looters in disguise, but he sent them on up to the center of town. They'd help—or steal what they could, if he was guessing wrong. One of the men had a retired military ID that helped to reassure him. Another was a CERT-trained volunteer from Cinci who had a card to prove it and a yellow stenciled helmet. Others were just citizens, and as long as they were middle-aged and couples, he worried little about their committing criminal acts. He sent a car full of teenagers away. They were probably good-intentioned, but he wouldn't take the chance—or, for that matter, put them in the way of injury.

Strangest of all were disaster tourists. People "just wanted to see." He pointed out the lights were out, there were deadly dangers, and that they'd get in the way of rescuers, but none of that seemed to convince them. After a few tries with each at politely explaining the rationale for their turning around, he put on his no-nonsense face and said, "If you go in there, you're at risk of being shot as a looter. Turn around." He couldn't stop them from sneaking in on a minor road, but he hoped he deterred some of them. Ghouls.

He said to Jackson, "It isn't just that it's creepy they want to come and stare. But they could see it all better if they sat home and watched it on TV."

"Like a Bengals game," Jackson said, which Greg thought a very odd comparison.

Either everyone else in the world was going crazy, or he was. Maybe a little of both.

When he was radioed and told to go downtown, he handed over the roadblock to Jackson and drove south first, far enough to get a cell signal. His aunt told him the results of the MRI.

"They say there's minor swelling."

"And that means?"

"He says it could be worse. They won't do anything, just wait and see for now. But he says if things change, they may need to do surgery. He needs your consent."

"He should do what he has to."

"He needs your signature, I mean."

"Shit." Greg thought. "What would they do for a child who was unidentified?" Wait until all the legal i's had been dotted?

"I have no idea, Greg."

"I'm sorry. I don't mean to complain to you. I appreciate what you're doing for us."

"You're like a son to me, Greg. And I adore Holly. You know that."

"Do—do whatever you can do. Tell him he has my permission. And I'll come in tomorrow to sign forms. Have them ready for me."

"I'll tell him."

He made the call to his ex-wife. It was after ten here. Eleven in Atlanta.

"It's Greg."

"I'm a little busy—"

"Kimberly, we had a tornado here."

"Oh?" She didn't sound very interested.

"Holly's in the hospital, with a head wound."

There was a long wait, and he wondered if he had lost the signal. But she finally said, "Is it serious?"

"She's in the *hospital*. Unconscious since it happened. Her skull is cracked. So, yes, it's serious."

"I'm sorry."

"What the fuck is wrong with you? Your daughter is critically injured, and you—" He ran out of words.

"Greg."

"What?" he snapped.

"I'm pregnant."

That would have made him feel something—a lot of things—

if the day hadn't numbed him. "Congratulations," he said in a flat tone.

"There've been a few complications. I can't fly, my doctor says."

"Then drive."

"I'm going to call you back. Ten minutes. Twenty at the most."

"But—" She had hung up. To the inside of the rental car, he said, "I really need this." What was wrong with her? Had the years away from Holly made her stop loving their daughter?

He had to get back to town, to his assignment. His ex would have to wait.

At the roadblock, Jackson was talking to someone in a new Lexus. Something in his posture told Greg he needed help. Greg pulled his rental car up and parked it on the shoulder.

The car held four frat-guy types, one of them clearly drunk. He suspected they all were. Without a breathalyzer, he couldn't ticket the driver for drunk driving. Without a jail with a drunk tank, he couldn't haul them in.

He looked over at Jackson. "What should we do?"

"I don't know. Take their keys?"

"Hey, man, you can't just strand us here!" said the driver.

Greg didn't want to. For one thing, they'd probably just walk into town on foot and cause trouble. "Get out of the car," he said.

He had all four of them walk the line and stand on one foot, recite the alphabet backward or give him multiples of 13. While he did, Jackson searched the car for drugs and liquor.

"Don't you need like a whatchamacallit for that?" the mouthiest of them complained.

"A gun?" Greg suggested. "Yeah, I have one of those."

Another one whispered, "Is anyone recording this?"

Greg tapped their names and driver's license numbers into his phone, and he'd check them later. He pointed to the one sober one of the lot, the one who had managed to stay on the line and remember the alphabet. He seemed okay to drive, though Greg would rather none of them did. Any other day, and he wouldn't allow it, not for a second. But with the police station gone, the rules had to change. "Drive slowly, don't stop for booze, get the first motel room you see. And do not come back to this town, or I'll find something to arrest you for."

When they were gone, Jackson said, "Hope they don't have a wreck."

He hated rich little assholes like that—had in college, did now. "As long as they don't hurt anyone else but themselves." He had no idea if he'd done the right thing. He realized his judgment had flown away about the time he'd lost his grip on Holly that afternoon. If he knew Jackson better, he'd let him make the decisions, even though the man no longer had a badge.

"Okay. I have to go back in now. Are you okay here?" he asked Jackson.

"I'll be fine. It's getting late. Traffic should slow down now, don't you think?"

"I hope." Without explaining it to Jackson, Greg drove south again until he got the cell signal.

There was a voice message from Kimberly. "Greg, I'm sorry. You know I care about Holly. But I have a chance now to have a baby—my own baby—and you know how important that is to me. Otherwise, I would come. You know I would. Keep me informed, would you? I hope everything is okay."

If Greg had any emotional energy left, he'd hate her. Adopting Holly had been more his idea than hers, yes. But he couldn't believe she wouldn't have bonded with her. Holly was 14 months old when she came to them, the child of a teenager who'd tried to raise her on her own and—bravely, Greg always thought—finally realized she could not. For Greg, it was love at first sight. For Kimberly, Holly had always felt like someone else's child. She hadn't said so, but it had been clear in every look, every touch. Kim could never stop Holly's fussing. Greg could. The baby had instinctively known who loved her most.

At the end of the marriage, Kimberly did talk honestly about the issue. She wanted her own children. Greg couldn't do that for her. He couldn't afford to pay for complicated fertility treatments. And to him, it didn't matter. Holly was his own. He couldn't see the difference between her and a child he had fathered biologically. Here was a child who needed him, a delightful toddler, bright and inquisitive and responsive to attention, and she was his. *His.* But not to Kimberly. Holly had been 75% of the reason for the divorce, though Kim's attitude had brought into focus for him several parts of her personality that he didn't like. Mostly, he saw that she had a cold and selfish streak.

And here it was again.

Holly might not have a mother, but she had a family, he reminded himself. She had him, she had Aunt Sherryl, and she had her paternal grandmother. Even Malika, for the past year of babysitting, had provided a stable, loving presence in her life.

He phoned his aunt again, while he still could, and woke her up. She whispered that they had a reclining chair in the room where she could nap if she needed to, and she was looking right at Holly as they spoke. No change. He thanked her and hung up.

He drove his car back through the checkpoint and into town.

Greg hadn't thought of Malika all day until now. He hoped she was okay. If he got a chance, he'd run past her mother's house and make sure.

He flipped on his radio to tell Dispatch he was coming in to be reassigned.

For most of the rest of the night, he worked on Main Street, along the path of the first tornado. His chief and the fire chief had decided time might be running out on injured people from the first tornado. They had a tent set up on the lawn of the former city hall, and they were conducting emergency operations out of it.

A volunteer firefighter he worked alongside said maybe the

first tornado's victims could be less badly hurt too. Greg wasn't sure. The gossip was, the first tornado had been an EF3, with winds of over 170, and the second an EF5, with winds well over 250 miles per hour. He was pretty sure it didn't matter if your house was knocked down by 150 or 300 mph winds. Either way, if a ton of house fell on you, you were done for.

"Yeah," said the guy, when he said this, "but the stronger winds will drive a rebar right through your gut. They had one of those up on Second Street, I heard."

"Thanks for the image," a woman working alongside said. She was in fatigues.

"Are you National Guard?" Greg asked her.

"Yeah. One tour in Afghanistan."

"I guess you've seen as bad as this."

"Not like seeing my own home destroyed."

"You live in town?" he asked.

"No, up in Eaton. But this could as easily have been Eaton, couldn't it? It's like my own neighborhood was leveled," she said. "Can you help me move this section of fencing here?"

"Sure," Greg said. Everyone had been issued heavy-duty work gloves by now.

They got the fence hauled over to the side of the road, came back, and shone flashlights onto the ground. No bodies. But there was an old wedding picture in a frame, from the 1970s, the glass over it broken, and the Guardsman picked it up and carried it over to a box.

She came back. "I shouldn't be taking the time to do that, I guess. But they say it might rain again. And you know someone wants that."

"If they're alive."

"If they aren't, might be someone else wants it even more."

"True enough," Greg said.

He stuck with the woman for the next few hours. She was a good work partner, physically strong, and efficient. Together, they were able to move heavier pieces than either could alone. There were entire framed walls, roof beams, and other debris that was going to need heavy equipment. When he checked in with Rosemary, about three a.m., he asked her when it was coming.

"We'll get more at dawn," she said. "Walk back over here, would you? I have a case of water and a case of soda for your crew. You can carry it back."

Greg realized then how thirsty he was. And hungry. How long had it been since he had eaten? As he walked back up Main Street toward the EOC, he tried to remember when he had eaten, and what, but his mind spun in circles and wouldn't slip into gear.

He found a woman in charge of the drinks. She introduced herself as Magarelli's mother.

"Do you know if there are any sandwiches or candy bars or whatever?"

"Someone is organizing breakfast for the first responders. Seven a.m., if all goes well. Probably just bologna sandwiches and coffee."

"That'd be great. I'm starting to lag."

"Long night," she agreed, and pointed him to the cases of drinks.

He hoisted two and made his way from this pool of light to the next, down a long dark stretch and to the third pool of light, which was his work area.

Everyone took a couple minutes to down a water. Then they got back to it.

By dawn, they had found three bodies and one seriously injured person who had been whisked off on a stretcher. They cleared one block and, after moving generator and lights, had cleared most of a second.

To say it was slow going was an understatement.

He hoped they'd do better in the daylight. He'd been computing. If the second tornado was five blocks wide, and it had stayed down all across town, which he thought it had, and if only one person had been home out of every five, on average? Every block, that still meant thirty people had been there. How many were dying right now, waiting for someone to find them? It could be hundreds. The job seemed overwhelming.

Of course, he knew, neighbors were helping to look. People on the south side of town, largely untouched, were searching for relatives and friends in the damaged areas.

Still, Greg wished he could be everywhere at once, helping. And he wished he could be with Holly too. For long minutes at a time, he was able to cut off that thought, but it kept drifting back to him. He hadn't checked on her in hours.

Rosemary called everyone in at dawn for a meeting. Greg saw Massey, who came over. "How's your kid?"

"Alive."

"Thank God for that."

"Yeah. I need to call in and check on her. How's your wife?"

"Fine. Helping with breakfast, in fact."

"So the tornado missed Springfield?"

"It actually caught the southern part of it, but by then everyone knew it was coming. She drove north out of the town to be sure, then circled back here."

The chief called for attention and used a bullhorn to make announcements. She encouraged everybody to go to the country club on the southwest edge of town to get fed. "I know most of you have double-shifted it already, but I'm asking you to work as many hours as you can stand, at least until sunset tonight, catching a catnap if you must, but hanging in for the town and for each other. We still have a chance at rescuing the injured." What she didn't say was that, after 24 hours, the chances of finding anyone alive were remote.

But they all knew it.

Rosemary passed out a pair of assignment sheets, printed by hand. Greg glanced at it and passed it along. He was getting reassigned to the northeast section of town, not a half-mile from his house. So, instead of eating, he'd try to call Sherryl again to get the news on Holly and, if he had time, check his own house.

Before she finished, the chief discussed phones. "We're hoping to get cell service back by sunset tonight, so we can go back to our regular communications."

There was a collective sigh of relief at that.

"Then tonight, from dusk to dawn, I'll split a shift so everyone can grab five hours' sleep. On your assignment sheet, you're either marked A or B group—A group works 8 to 1 a.m., B group from 1 to 6 a.m. I hope after that we'll have enough support from other agencies that we can get back to regular shifts."

He was assigned to his area of town today along with Higgins. When Rosemary was done, he went over and asked him how it was going.

"Seen some awful things," Higgins said.

"I know. My kid was hurt. I'm hoping to check in on her, so could you grab a sandwich or whatever is easy at the breakfast while I make that call?"

He was more sympathetic than Rosemary had been and agreed to meet him out at the site with the sandwich in a half-hour to forty-five, depending on how well organized things were at the country club. They agreed on a cross street to meet, and Greg made for his car again.

As dawn cast a rosy light, Greg drove toward the rising sun, his phone on, hunting for the first cell signal. When he had two bars on the phone, he pulled over and called his aunt. She asked him to hold, and he heard her say Holly's name. A seed of hope sprouted in his chest. Was she awake?

Sherryl came back on and said, "She seems the same. I called her name and patted her arm, told her you were calling, but she didn't respond at all."

Greg felt again the pull to go to his daughter. He couldn't. "Would you do me a favor and text an update to Kimberly every twelve hours? I'll text you her phone number."

"She's not coming?" his aunt said.

"No," he said, shortly. "I'm sorry, Aunt Sherryl, but I have to get to work now."

After sending the text, he stayed parked where he was and scrolled through text messages, finding one from his mother. He read it and texted back that it'd be best to phone Sherryl at the hospital. Next he spent a couple minutes looking at news of the tornado online at the *Enquirer* website. An overhead view showed the path of damage in Fidelity, with a center zone of utter destruction. The edges of that area had that weird tornado signature of a few houses nearly untouched in a block of razed homes. Maybe his was one. Flipping the phone off, he drove back in.

He got as close to his assignment as he could manage, but the roads were still strewn with dangerous debris and he had to park three blocks away on Oak, on a patch of street that had been swept up by responsible residents. He grabbed his car rental receipt, found a pen in the glove box, and wrote the word "POLICE" on the back of it, then stuck it in the front window.

The problem with agreeing to meet Higgins at the corner of Oak and Ninth was that there was no Oak and Ninth any more. Every street sign had been torn off, except for a rare post bent over, still stuck in concrete, that might have held anything from a cross street sign to a stop sign to a "slow children" sign. Every post looked like every other one, and he had to guess when three blocks had passed.

Looking around, he realized they were lucky to live in a town that had basements, at least in all the older homes. No doubt it had cut the fatalities in half.

At the heart of the damaged area, even the roads themselves were destroyed. He stopped and asked a couple rummaging through wreckage if that was their house. The man, seeing Greg's vest and badge, got out his wallet and handed over his driver's license. "I'm glad you're looking out for looters."

Greg nodded and checked the address. He was a half-block north of where he should meet his partner. "Are you finding anything?"

"Not much," said the man. "I guess the things we really want, like the car title and birth certificates, are blown away from here. We've found some other people's photos, which we're picking up."

"I imagine there'll be some sort of social media thing," said the woman, "linking people with found objects."

"That's true," said Greg. "Good luck, both of you. I have to go look for survivors." He almost said, "Have a good day," but that'd be about the stupidest thing he'd said since this happened. How could you have a good day at a time like this, with your home razed and all your belongings scattered over a square mile? He hoped they hadn't lost anyone they loved.

He hoped he hadn't.

Then he remembered Jim had died. They hadn't been as close as he and Sherryl were, but he'd been a good guy. That death seemed so distant. Greg knew he was emotionally shut down, as you had to be at a bad car accident or shotgun suicide or any of the other horrors police work made you see.

All his worry and grief was focused into a narrow beam, aimed at his own daughter. And even that, he had to try and forget in order to do his job.

Higgins was twenty minutes late, but he had a large duffel bag with him. Out of it, he pulled two sandwiches wrapped in paper napkins that he handed to Greg. He searched his pockets for two paper containers of marmalade. Greg tore them open and piled them on one sandwich—hard-fried egg and bacon on biscuit— and ate the first sandwich in three bites. By the time he was unwrapping the second, Higgins had gotten out a bottle of flavored iced tea.

"It's not coffee," he said, by way of apology.

"It's great. Thanks." Greg unwrapped the other sandwich, but before he took a bite said, "Was it crazy down at the country club?"

"They had it organized pretty well, several tables set up with food and coffee and orange juice, and then another couple long tables with these kinds of sandwiches already slapped together. It was crowded, and they may have run out of food before the last of the fire or Guard guys got there."

Greg chewed and swallowed. "I worked with a Guardswoman last night. She was on top of things."

"Yeah, I guess most of them are pretty good at this."

"I think she'd seen worse."

Higgins looked around. "I can't imagine there could *be* worse."

Greg finished his second sandwich and washed it down with most of the bottle of tea. "Let's get to it."

"I have some equipment in my bag. Rope, pry bar, bolt cutters."

"That's great. I have my gloves around here somewhere." Greg patted himself and found his work gloves in a back pocket.

"How's your kid?"

"Alive," said Greg. "Let's try and find someone else who is."

"Roger that," Higgins said.

They decided to start with the first people they could see, asking them if they were looking for people—they were not—and then quizzing them about neighbors. They'd seen three of their neighbors yesterday evening, working on clearing their property, and they pointed out the house sites where they knew nothing about how the residents had fared.

Greg and Higgins started with those. Each of them had learned different procedures working in different groups yesterday, and they combined the best ideas to get through the first block quickly. They ran across a living cat sitting on top of a battered electric stove, but that was the only sign of life. They moved south from there, finding three families looking through the debris field in the next block. Again, they questioned them and checked ID.

Over the course of the morning, they worked in a spiral around Oak and Tenth, covering five full blocks in all. They found three bodies, one crushed beyond recognition, and a severed leg.

"Hope no one is still looking for that," said Higgins. Gallows humor.

Greg got the image of a person with one leg, searching the neighborhood for it by hopping around. "I'm getting tired," he said, to keep himself from laughing at the sick humor his mind was using to cope.

"I could use a break. I'm hungry again. I wonder what we're supposed to do for lunch."

"You know," Greg said, "we could check my house. If there's anything left of it, if by some miracle it's standing, you can eat all you want out of the fridge before it goes bad."

"Man, you don't know yet if your house is still here?"

"No," said Greg, arching his back and rubbing at the aching muscles.

"It's near here?"

Greg had to think about where they were. "About three blocks to the west, one north." He stretched his arms overhead. "What about you? Family, house okay?"

"We live southside. If you need a place to stay—"

Greg shook his head. "My aunt's house made it through, but thanks."

They made their way through the increasingly crowded streets, stopping people to ask for ID. A few had none—or claimed they had none. In one case, a neighbor vouched for the person. In the other, Higgins gave a short lecture on looting and souvenir hunting, but the way the person just numbly nodded made Greg think they were legit.

One man asked, "Have you seen my fence?"

Greg and Higgins exchanged glances at that. "I'm not sure I

could tell your fence from any other," Greg said, as gently as he could. "You might even have a hard time."

"It was brand new," the man said, and then he wandered back to his search without another word.

"Shell-shocked," said Higgins, watching him go.

Greg couldn't disagree.

On Greg's street, there was a crew of three women and a man who admitted to not being local. One woman said, "We're trying to find photo albums, baby pictures, that sort of thing. It's supposed to rain tomorrow again, so if any of that can be saved, it'll be today."

Another woman said, "We just want to help. Any way we can."

Higgins and Greg exchanged a glance. Greg shrugged. "We'll take your names, if you don't mind."

They didn't protest and offered up driver's licenses.

When they were out of earshot, Higgins said to Greg, "I hope we didn't just make a mistake."

"How much more damage can they do?"

"Maybe they'll find diamonds or gold."

"Maybe." Greg didn't know if they could stop that sort of thing from happening. He pointed. "This is my place, I think."

They were standing in front of a decimated area. Nothing stood to help him identify his house.

"I'm sorry, man."

"I'm not upset," Greg said.

"Why not?" Higgins asked. "I would be."

"If Holly is okay, I'd happily trade the house for that."

"I wish it worked that way."

Greg knew it didn't. But he couldn't mourn a TV or a spare uniform or a box of zip drive discs from his college computer. Beds and chairs and plates could be replaced. His house insurance was paid up. If they didn't screw him too badly, he could rebuild.

But without Holly, would he want to? He swallowed past a

tight throat.

"Do you want to look for anything? Pictures, or...?"

"No. Not while there are still people who might be saved."

"We haven't seen any today."

"Last one I saw was in the middle of the night. How about you?"

"Around 11, I think, last night—we pulled someone out of a smashed car."

They did not look at each other. Both were probably thinking the same thing. With every hour, the chances of finding anyone still alive were fading.

"Let's radio in to see if they've organized something for lunch. Then work our way back from here to where we stopped."

"Sounds good."

They were sent to the Central school location to meet Guardsmen who had food for the rescue workers.

"Easier to walk, or drive?" asked Higgins.

"Either way, but...."

"What?"

"I'd just as soon not go there. Would you mind carrying back a meal to me again? I'll keep looking around here while you're gone."

Greg did all the rescue work he could alone, avoiding lifting or moving anything too heavy. He helped a single woman, middle-aged, move some of the debris from her home site.

"It's like moving day all over again," she said, puffing with the effort of moving a king-sized mattress.

"Hadn't thought of that, but you're right," he said. "Is this your bed?"

"Nope," she said, and bent to comb through a pile of broken kitchen things that had been beneath it. "These are all mine. They were all in a cabinet."

There was no cabinetry around. Seemed odd something light like these dishes would be here while a whole row of kitchen cabinets were gone.

It was odd, but hardly the oddest thing he had seen that morning. All over there were freakish sights. Cars crushed better than the junkyard could do it. A fork driven into the side of a refrigerator. Two-by-sixes shoved through car doors. He had found a small birdcage earlier, its door closed. The bird was missing, but the birdseed was miraculously still in the little plastic cup. He wondered if the bird had been out of the cage when it started, or if the wind had blown it right through the bars of the cage.

Higgins returned with sandwiches wrapped in paper and cans of Vernors. They found a couple of pressed concrete blocks, and used them as chairs. They stripped off their work gloves and ate the sandwiches in silence.

Greg's was salami, ham, and provolone with pepperoncinis and oil and vinegar on a hard white roll. Salty and rich and filling. A couple of bags of crushed potato chips had come with them. He tried to tear his open, but it wouldn't budge. Higgins offered up the bolt cutters, which seemed overkill, but there was no way to open a bag of chips without some tool. Upending the bag into his mouth, he ate the chip fragments and washed it down with the ginger ale.

"Back to it," he said, standing up. Damn, but his weapon was feeling heavy on his hip. The radio counterbalanced it to an extent. He re-cinched the belt. He swore he had lost weight in just a day.

Higgins was a few bites behind. He crammed the last of his sandwich into his mouth, wiped his hands on his pants, dusted the concrete dust off the seat of his pants, adjusted his belt, and pulled on his gloves again.

They followed the street they were on northward. This time, some of the people they ran into were unauthorized, disaster tourists taking video. They sent them on their way. Higgins was about to chase a couple of other men off when Greg recognized the guy with the camera.

"Wait," he said. "Aren't you the storm chasers?"

"Yeah," said the shorter of the two, the one without the camera. "Captain T at your service. That's T for tornado."

"You have a real name?"

"Joel," he said, a little sheepishly.

"I'm the one you ran into outside of town yesterday." Yesterday? It seemed like a year ago.

"Oh right. Sorry about your car, man. We'll pay for the damage."

Greg waved it off. "It was in the second tornado. That little dent isn't one percent of the damage it has now."

"Wow. But you made it?"

"Barely. Underground." He didn't want to think of it again. If he could get those moments when Holly was snatched from his arms erased from his mind, he'd have the surgery or take the pill or suffer whatever indignity to get it erased.

"You okay?" said the chaser.

"Fine. Why aren't you guys chasing today?"

"It's only spinning out a few, F1s at worst, in Pennsylvania. Yesterday was a bona fide outbreak, a swarm of F5s from Indiana right on through Ohio. You got the worst of it."

"Lucky us," said Higgins. "I get that you're experienced at it. But you still shouldn't be in here."

"You shouldn't bother the victims," Greg said. "Their lives are hard enough right now."

"Sometimes, it helps them to talk about it."

It wouldn't help him. "Just stay out at the edges, okay?"

"Can we interview you two?" said the videographer.

"We have to try and find survivors," said Higgins.

"Maybe later," said Greg. "If you guys happen to get any video of crimes—looting, in particular—would you let us have that?"

"Sure."

"If you do that, then I'll give you an interview later. About sunset, if you're still around."

"We will be."

Higgins and Greg went on to the next street, booted out more disaster tourists, and started hunting through the rubble for survivors again. This was one of those areas like on the overhead view, where a few houses still stood.

Higgins pointed out the curved path of destruction. "I think that's one of those little twisters that you see on the side of the big ones."

"Yeah?" Greg squinted and tried to imagine that.

"I was out of both of them, but working on the south side when the second one hit. We could see it really clearly across the damage zone, but we couldn't do a damned thing about it." He kicked at a fourteen-foot chunk of lumber, a four-by-four. "Help me lift this. Watch the nails there."

"Always," Greg said, thinking about the puncture in his palm, which was still sore, hot and achy. "Damn," he said. "I forgot to get a tetanus shot at the hospital." Then he shook his head. "Nah, it would have taken forever. The place was a zoo." He thought of Holly lying there in the hospital. Thank God for Sherryl. He wondered if Holly was awake yet, asking for him. He wondered if she had taken a turn for the worse. What if she was in surgery?

"Hey. You with me?"

"Sorry. I got distracted," Greg said, and turned his attention back to the board. They lifted together and moved the board to the edge of the street.

They both got down on their hands and knees and peered into an opening that the board's removal had left. Higgins got out his Maglite and flipped it on.

Greg saw a curved shape. It took a moment to recognize it as a human arm. "I think we have another body."

Then, to his amazement, the arm moved. "Holy shit," he said. "Survivor."

Higgins began tossing lightweight debris over his shoulder.

Boards, pipes, and bits of furniture blocked their way.

Greg glanced over his shoulder and saw more disaster tourists wandering up the block, a couple in their 20s, shooting video on a phone. "Hey, you two!" he said, waving them over.

"What?"

"Put that phone down and get over here," he said.

The man with the camera hesitated, but the woman came.

"You live here?"

"South of town about a mile." She named the nicer trailer park in town.

"You're being recruited as volunteers, both of you, for a minute. As we clear this junk out, carry it ten feet away. Get it out of our way."

The man lifted the camera phone again.

"Put that damn thing down, or I'm going to—to confiscate it," he said, deciding that sounded more professional than "cram it up your ass," which is what he wanted to say.

"Gee, I was just—"

"Just help. A life depends on it."

The woman was already picking up a pair of bricks and walking them several feet away. She dropped them with a clank.

"Watch out for nails. Any board, assume nails, screws, splinters. And watch for broken glass," Greg said. He waited until the man pocketed his phone, then he worked with Higgins to clear enough debris to allow them access to the injured person.

They had to move a pile of stuff about eight feet by four feet before light shone in and struck the injured person, allowing Greg to see it was a woman. She was so covered with dirt and mud and smaller debris that he couldn't guess at her age. She was on her side, her face half-hidden. "Ma'am?" he called down. "Can you hear us?"

No answer.

"Can you reach her?" he asked Higgins.

"Hang on to my belt. I'll see." He pulled a piece of particle board over and lay on it, then wriggled forward until his top half was hanging over the open space. He reached down, and Greg had to pull back to keep him from sliding in on top of the woman.

"Not quite," he said, scrambling to his feet. "We have to clear out a little more, and then there's a space I think one of us can stand. I think this is a crawlspace she's in, not a basement. There's concrete under her, but it's only a few feet down."

Higgins pushed the particle board back and began pulling more bits of junk out of the hole. A lamp base, a Big Wheel truck, a satchel. Greg worked by his side, pulling out a computer printer, a saucepan, and bits of aluminum too mangled to identify.

Behind him, the tourist couple talked quietly together as they cleared the debris farther back.

"I think I can get down," said Higgins. "Can you lower me?"

"I think I'm lighter than you," said Greg. "Mind doing it the other way?"

"Fine." He turned to the woman. "Hey, see that duffle bag over there by the street? That's mine. There's a first aid kit in it. Bring that over in case we need it, would you?"

"Sure," said the woman, hurrying off. The man came around to watch as Higgins lowered Greg into the hole, feet first.

As he was lowered slowly, he felt with the toes of his shoes for the concrete, making sure he wasn't landing on some part of the injured woman. "Okay, let go." He fell the last few inches and felt his soles slap the hard concrete of the crawlspace. He turned and bent over the woman. He was blocking his own light. Fumbling his flashlight out of his belt, he turned it on and shone it on her face.

"How is she?"

"Not moving any more. I'm checking," Greg said. He felt the neck for a pulse. Her skin was caked with dried mud. He had to flake a bunch of it off. He tried again for a pulse, moved his fingers, tried again, flaked more mud off, and finally felt the beat of a heart. "She's alive," he called up.

"Responsive?"

"Not yet," he said. "We need EMT, rescue. I don't want to move her."

"Visible injuries?"

"I'm seeing scratches, a bit of dried blood." He picked up his flashlight and ran the beam along the body. "Nothing obvious."

"Try to get her to respond."

Greg shone the flashlight in her face. With his other hand, he tapped her on the shoulder. "Ma'am? Ma'am, can you hear me?" Nothing. He leaned down and barked, "Hey!"

She moved her arm. Not much, maybe an inch, but it was something.

"What's your name?" he said.

No answer.

Greg looked up and called to Higgins. "She moved again, but she's not talking." Just then a mini landslide of dirt fell into his face. He turned and spat.

"Damn you!" Higgins was saying. "Back off. And get that damned phone—no, wait."

Greg heard Higgins stomping around, then a scuffle. The sightseer's voice saying, "Hey, you can't do that."

"I'm confiscating this. Now go home."

"It's my phone."

"It'll be at the police station, waiting for you. When there is a police station again."

"You can't—"

"I can and I have. Now both of you, get. And let the grownups do their grownup jobs."

"I'll report you!"

"Knock yourself out," Higgins said.

Greg saw his shadow, and then he was leaning over. "You hear that?"

"Yeah. I'd have done the same."

"I'll probably get a reprimand."

"Join the club. Rosemary's pissed at me too. EMTs here yet?"

His shadow moved. "No sign of them. You want me to help you out of there?"

"I'm not able to do anything for her, so I may as well clear out so the EMTs can get in quicker."

"Here, give me your hands."

Greg stretched up as far as he could and Higgins got hold of his wrists. He was strong, bigger and broader than Greg, and all Greg had to do was suffer the pain in his shoulders while he was dragged up. His foot hit something solid and he was able to put it down to take the strain off both of them as he was hauled up the last few inches.

"Whew!"

"Good job," Greg said. "You must lift weights."

"Not a bit. My girlfriend has horses, so I throw some bales of hay around every weekend."

"I didn't know that. Did her horses make it okay through the storm?"

"Hers did, but she's out today helping rescue other lost animals. Or recovering their bodies and trying to get the information to the owner."

"That's nice." He tried to imagine his ex doing something like that and failed. He had to admit, he had chosen a wife badly. And now Holly had to pay.

He looked around and saw a new couple wandering down the street. "I'll check them," he said, walking over to intercept them.

The man glanced at him, said something to the woman, and they pivoted and took off running, the woman clasping a big shoulder bag to her hip.

"Stop! Police!" he said. As if they didn't know by his vest. Over his shoulder, he called, "Wait for the EMT. I'm in pursuit."

"I'll radio it in," Higgins said.

Greg took off after the couple. They were having trouble negotiating the debris-filled street. Trouble was, so was he.

Seemed like everything underfoot was trying to trip him up.

The couple was more than a half a block ahead of him. They turned left, up Seventh Street. When he made the turn, he saw they had gotten even farther ahead through a clear patch. He put on speed and raced after them.

The gap between them decreased. He was thinking he'd catch up in another half-block when a resident stood up on the right side from looking through the ruins of his house, glanced at the scene, and pulled a gun out, a replica—or authentic—19th century Colt, from the looks of it, and aimed it at the fleeing suspects.

"Don't!" Greg cried, just as the man shot.

Either he was a crappy shot or a very good one trying to miss, for the round seemed to pass in front of the couple and they skidded to a halt—or the man did. The woman skidded and went down as if she were sliding into second base.

Greg stopped, drew out his service Glock, and yelled, "Drop your weapon, sir."

The man didn't drop it, but he lowered it. "Are they looters?"

"I don't know what they are yet. Please, drop your weapon, or I can't move toward them."

The man looked at the couple, back at Greg, shrugged, and set the big pistol on the ground.

"Step away from it," Greg said.

Just then, the male suspect regained his feet and began to run again.

Greg knew the regulations, but he thought, Screw it, and he fired his weapon into a mattress not far from the woman. "Both of you, stop. Hands on your head."

The man did, but the woman's bag was caught on something and she was trying to wrestle it free.

"Ma'am, I'm losing patience. Hands on your head, now." He glanced to the Colt owner, to make sure he hadn't decided to involve himself again. He stood with folded arms and an angry expression.

Greg had three points of concern too far away from each other. He circled around to the left of the woman, at the same time telling the man, "Slowly, you walk back over here to your associate."

By the time he had, Greg had the two of them and the gun-toting citizen in the same general direction, but not in a straight line. He needed to be able to shoot any one of them if, God forbid, things went south.

"Okay, you two, get down on your bellies. Hands on the back of your head."

"Us?" the man said in a fake innocent voice.

"You," said Greg, through gritted teeth. He had never shot anyone in the line of duty, but he was sorely tempted to right now. "Faster. I'm tired and I'm in a bad mood."

They got down and Greg cautiously made his way forward, keeping the gun trained on them. Out of the corner of his eye, the man took a step toward his Colt.

"Don't. Sir, stay where you are."

"I could help."

"You're not helping. Just back away from that weapon. Let me do my job."

"I know what I'm doing. I have training."

"Then you should know not to interfere with me right now."

The man shrugged, stepped back, and folded his arms again. Greg saw a group of four or five citizens come around the corner of the next street. "Everybody keep back."

They stopped. Greg inched forward until he was at the fleeing couple. He fished in his belt for plastic cuffs and got first the man's then the woman's hands immobilized behind their backs. He leaned down to release the woman's bag from where it was hung up on a twisted bed frame. He unzipped it and looked inside. He was expecting jewels, gold, guns, small high-ticket items.

What he saw was mail, dirty envelopes. What the hell?

He glanced at the couple again. The man was muttering something to his accomplice, so he yanked him upright and pushed him ten feet away, then got him down on his belly again. Greg went back and looked again at the contents of the bag. He found two driver's licenses—one of them from this neighborhood, one of them from west of town. A half-used checkbook. And mail. He looked inside one uncanceled envelope and saw a check written to an insurance company in a shaky hand. Probably an older person who didn't know how to pay bills online. Another envelope held a brand new credit card, from the feel of it.

"You're identity thieves?" he said to the woman. "That's the scam?"

She said nothing.

At that moment, Massey and Evans came around the corner at a run. They approached at a trot and Greg said, "These are looters. Identity theft seems to be their thing." He described the brief chase and what was in the bag.

Massey asked, "You want us to take them?"

"Yeah, but—where?" The jail was destroyed as well as City Hall and the station.

Massey hauled the man to his feet. "Sheriff's deputies will transport them to County."

"Right," he said. "Don't forget the bag of evidence."

Evans was already pushing the woman to the west.

"You'll have paperwork to fill out," said Massey, "as soon as there are forms again."

"Yeah. I bet they're here by the end of the day."

"Anything else you need help with?"

Greg glanced at the Colt owner, thought about it, then shook his head. "No. Everything's copasetic."

"How's your kid?"

Greg felt a wave of guilt. During the excitement, she had left his thoughts for a moment. "Still unconscious. I need to check in with my aunt soon."

"She's with her?"

"Yeah."

"That's good. I'm glad you have someone." He nodded at Greg and led the man away.

Greg went over to where the Colt lay, cracked it open and removed the remaining rounds. He walked it over to the man. "This yours?"

"It is. I'm a collector."

"Real, or replica?"

"It's real. First generation, 1879, Army issue."

"And if I asked you for proof it was yours?"

The man opened his mouth, shut it, looked around and gave an expressive shrug. "I suppose I couldn't prove it. Not right now."

"Were you aiming to hit those people, or not?"

"Trying to stop them. Looked like you needed the help."

Greg handed him back the empty weapon. "I appreciate the thought. But let the authorities do the shooting from now on."

"They were looters?"

"Looks like it."

"Then I'm a little sorry I didn't aim for them."

"I understand the sentiment, but I'm not the person to say that to."

Finally, the fellow looked sheepish.

"This was your place?" Greg asked.

"Yeah. Mess, ain't it?"

"Mine looks the same."

"Sorry to hear it."

"Good luck finding more of your stuff." Greg raised a hand

and walked away. He could arrest the guy, but he sympathized. You lose everything, and here comes someone trying to steal the bits you have left. Seems pretty normal to want to shoot at them. Nobody was dead, and the right people got arrested. The rest of it, he could let go.

He hadn't heard it arrive, but a small fire truck had managed to get in to the street where he had left Higgins. They were hauling a stretcher out just as he came up.

"What's the news?"

"She's still alive. What's the news with you? Catch them all right?"

"I did. Massey and Evans hauled them away."

"Looters?"

"Looks like they were going for documents, for identity theft."

"Kinda smart. For the next week or two, all these lives will be in disarray. It'd be hard to determine who is the real Greg Duncan."

"Tell me about it."

"I've read about people faking their identity to get Red Cross emergency funds too."

Greg looked around the utter devastation and thought of all the people who did need help. "Lowest of the low."

"I hope there's a Hell. Doubt it, but it'd sure be nice to think they're headed there."

Greg watched the EMTs getting the woman loaded onto the truck, made sure they didn't need any help, and took the opportunity to pull out his cell phone. No signal, still. "Hey, can we take a break for fifteen minutes? Maybe catch a ride out with these guys?"

"You need to piss or something?"

That wouldn't be a bad idea either. "I was wanting to try and call in to the hospital again. My daughter."

"Right. Okay, sure. I'll radio in."

The EMTs let them climb aboard and got them out of the

debris field and to the rental car. Higgins suggested they drive up to a gas station convenience store first, so they could get something to drink. There, Greg was able to get through to Sherryl. No change with Holly. "Tell her I love her," he said, his throat closing on the last words.

"I will. And she knows, honey. She knows."

Chapter 15

Malika woke a long time later. Her mother was asleep in a chair. She stretched cautiously and her legs twanged in pain. "Shoot," she said.

"Malika?" Adam.

She turned her head and saw him in the dim light. She reached for his hand at the same time he reached for hers.

"Are you okay?"

"I am."

"Doesn't hurt?"

"A little. But they're keeping me doped up."

"And you hating drugs like you do."

"I'm feeling more kindly about them now."

He smiled, and it warmed her all over.

"Thank you," she said. "For helping me back there."

"Nothing I'd rather do," he said, and he winced. "That came out wrong. I'd rather you hadn't been hurt at all."

"I understood you. And thank you for that too. For being loyal. I probably don't deserve it."

He was shaking his head. "Never mind that right now. Just get well."

"Is your family okay? With the tornado?"

"Totally. Everyone is fine, but we lost our satellite dish and some shingles off the roof."

"I'm sorry."

"It's nothing compared to other people. It missed our house by a block and a half. But you should see Fidelity. Some of it is smashed flat."

"You brought my mom?" She turned her head, and her mother was still sleeping.

"My mom brought us both and talked the nurses into letting me in here with your mom. My mom will be back in the morning, at visiting hours." He squeezed her hand tighter. "I'm so glad you're awake."

"I guess they know I don't have good insurance by now," Malika said.

"I don't think it matters."

It did. She knew there was no sense in explaining it to Adam. What would happen to her would happen, with her having no say-so in it. They'd kick her out or not.

"And if it did matter, I'd start an online campaign for you, and get all your medical bills paid."

"It's okay," she said. She didn't want to talk about money or the internet or anything at all. Just having him here and holding her hand was enough.

"Do you want me to wake your mom up?"

"In a minute," she said. "How was she? When you told her?"

"You know your mom."

She had to smile at that. "Yes."

"She depends on you a lot."

Also not news to Malika.

"If you need to, while you're recovering, you can stay with us. My mom said it was okay."

"She's nice, your mom."

"About important stuff, she definitely comes through."

They shared a moment of quiet, and then Malika gathered up

her courage. "Adam, you know...."

"What?"

"I still love you."

He closed his eyes and raised her hand and kissed it. She felt a tear drop before she saw that he was crying.

"I'm sorry that I hurt you."

He dropped her hand to swipe at his face. "We'll talk in a few days, Malika. Right now you save your strength to get better."

"Did you hear what's wrong with me?"

"No. They talked to your mother alone about that."

Malika gave him a brief explanation of the kidney issue. "But they told me I'd walk again."

"That's great. And I'll do whatever you need for you. Get your assignments from school. Carry you if I need to."

She laughed. "I appreciate the chivalry, but it isn't necessary."

"I'll do anything you need. Anything. I'm your friend, no matter what."

He was. She knew they wouldn't be together after college, more than likely. She knew the statistics about high school romance. But he was her first lover, and her first love. She hoped they'd be friends forever. "I guess I'm ready to face my mom. And while I talk to her, could you hunt down a nurse and get me some more drugs?"

"You're becoming a regular doper," he said.

"For a day or two, I think I'll give it a try."

He got up, kissed her forehead, and then backed off. Asking permission first with a look, he leaned in and gave her a tender kiss on the lips.

She was able to forget the pain while he was kissing her.

* * *

Greg had finally ended the longest shift of his life and was in Sherryl's house, showering and changing into some of Jim's old clothes. They were at least a size too big. He took a moment, standing in front of the closet, to think about Jim and his kind, patient ways. He had been a good husband to Sherryl, and she would miss him. Every day, she had gone to that nursing home. He wondered what would fill her hours now.

And if Holly died, what would fill his life?

Nothing. Nothing could ever replace a Holly-sized absence. She was his heart, his life. Without her, he'd be like a boat without rudder, sails, oar, or engine, stuck in a gale on the ocean.

He was bone tired. He was assaulted by images of bodies and body parts. He wanted nothing more than the oblivion of twelve hours of sleep. But he locked up the house and drove to the hospital to be with his daughter.

He had negotiated an evening shift the next day from the chief, who seemed to have forgotten her earlier irritation with him in the face of all the work she had to do. She looked even more worn out than he felt, he mused, as he drove down to Cincinnati. New to the job, probably feeling the pressure of being the first woman police chief, and with a huge disaster on her hands. She had given him a whole day shift to be with Holly, so he was thinking more kindly of her. He'd have to nap at the hospital.

He also thought about the new card that was in his wallet. It had come from the woman Guardsman he had worked with that first night, the hard worker. She had said, "I know this isn't a great time for you. But if you ever want to get together for coffee," and handed it to him.

Any other time, he would have been thrilled. Right now it was far down his priority list. He had to be with Holly. He had to keep his job. And he had to be kinder to his aunt, who had lost her husband today—no, yesterday.

As he drove into the hospital parking lot, he felt sick—sick at heart, sick with fear. Again, he had a hard time finding the ward Holly was on, but he finally stumbled upon it. He stopped to show his ID to the nurse and went back to Holly's room.

* * *

She looked so tiny and helpless and pale lying there. He kissed both her cheeks and laid one of his against it. He remembered the last normal morning, when she'd complained about his scratchy face. Her face was so smooth, and soft, and perfect. She'd barely begun life. It wouldn't be fair if it was snatched away from her now.

He looked at the machines, keeping track of her heart beat and blood pressure and brain function. Her head was erratically shaved, and leads were attached that led to the machines. He looked at all the readouts and had no idea what they were telling him. At least all of them were changing all the time. That must be good.

He knew he was snatching at any sign of hope, but it didn't stop him from snatching.

His aunt was dozing in the chair, pushed back all the way. That it looked comfortable alleviated a spoonful of his guilt for asking her to stay here.

He let her sleep and pulled up the straight chair tucked into a corner of the room. It was as uncomfortable as it looked. Good— maybe it'd serve as his penance for letting Holly be ripped out of his arms. He should have never let it happen. He tried to be a good father, but all the good he had done in the past six years had been erased by his failure in the tornado.

* * *

He woke with a start.

"Sorry," his aunt's voice said. She took her hand off his shoulder and stood in front of him, waiting for him to become oriented.

"I must have dozed off."

"You need sleep."

The room had no windows, so he had no idea how long he'd been out. He checked his watch. He'd been asleep for a while.

He stretched out kinks in his neck and went to check Holly. No change he could see. He turned back to Sherryl, who had taken a seat in the hard chair. "You must want to go home."

"When do you need to work again?"

"I should leave about 3:30 this afternoon."

"Okay, I will take some time in the morning then. Check the house."

"I was just there. Everything is okay."

"Thanks."

"I took some of Jim's clothes."

"I noticed. You look like a teenager wearing those oversized clothes."

"I'm so sorry, Sherryl. You must be devastated. And I haven't been supportive at all."

"You have your own worries. And Jim—well, maybe it was a blessing, all things considered."

"I know you'll miss him."

"I was missing him already." She gave him a sad smile. "I'm going to see a funeral director today. I imagine there's a line. No hurry on his cremation, as far as I'm concerned. I don't even mind if we have to go to Eaton or Dayton to have it."

"Dayton was hit too."

"Or down here. Wherever." She frowned. "Can I ask you something?"

"Whatever you want."

"I need to know if I committed a crime."

"You?" He smiled for the first time in a day. "I doubt it seriously."

"Jim didn't just die. I let him die."

"I'm sorry. What do you mean? How could you have stopped it?"

"I could have gotten help. But he asked me not to. He had a

moment of clarity. And he said he wanted to be let go." Her eyes filled with tears. "So I let him go. Someone even came by and asked, and I said he was gone." She used her blouse to dab away the one tear that had spilled over. "Does that make me a killer?"

He took her hand. "Not under the law, and not under moral law, either. I think it just makes you brave."

"No, not brave. I feel guilty."

"I wish you wouldn't. Tell me how it happened."

By the time she was halfway through the story, he was shaking his head. Nothing in what she said was changing his mind.

"Look," he said. "You know what triage is, right?"

"Of course."

"If you had pulled in an EMT or doctor, they would have probably passed him by anyway. I saw it out there myself." Luckily, he hadn't made any of those decisions himself, like black-tagging someone who was still breathing. But had the day's events changed just a mite, had the fire station been destroyed, he might have had to make that call himself. "You didn't do anything wrong."

"He said it's what he wanted."

"Then do him the honor of believing it. He's at peace now."

She brushed it away. "I'm sorry. You're worried about Holly, and I'm troubling you with my moral crisis."

"I have room in my heart for both of you."

"Why don't you take the reclining chair. I've had enough rest, and you can sleep until the doctors come in. The nurse said it would be early."

"You'll wake me if anything happens?"

"I will."

After checking Holly one last time, he sank gratefully into the soft chair. Worry should have kept him awake, but physical exhaustion from hauling debris around had taken its toll. He sunk into oblivion.

When next he woke, it was to his aunt saying his name

urgently. His eyes popped open and he lurched to his feet. "What?"

"Holly's eyes are open."

He jumped to her side to see. Her eyes were open. He looked into them and said, "Holly. Honey, it's me."

There was no reaction at all. He waved his hand in front of her face, but her eyes didn't follow them. *Lights on, nobody home.* The awful phrase went through his mind before he could censor it. Anger at himself made his voice sharp. "Holly. Wake up!"

She frowned.

"This has to be good, right?" he said to his aunt. "It has to."

"I'm sure it is. I'm going to go get the nurse."

With so many leads and lines going in and out of her, he couldn't shake her. But he wanted to. He wanted to shake her awake. "C'mon, kiddo. Let's go," he said. "I love you. I need you, baby."

The nurse came in then and shooed him aside. She checked Holly, and she checked the readouts at the machines.

When she was done, Greg said, "Is she okay?"

"She's fine."

"Is she going to wake up?"

"I'll let the doctor talk to you."

"Why don't you just tell me? You probably know every bit as well as he does!" Greg fought to keep his anger under control.

"I'm sorry, but I really can't. I understand how frustrated you are. How afraid. I see that every day, and I really do know."

She probably did, at that. She'd probably seen worse. "I'm sorry. I didn't mean to raise my voice."

"I'll call the neurologist right now."

Greg checked his watch. Probably she'd be waking the doctor, but he was no doubt used to it. Greg felt a sudden—and not entirely welcome—rush of affinity for the nurse and doctor. They had similar enough jobs to his own—never seeing people at their best, woken out of sound sleeps, having to calm down hysterical people. The nurse was already out of the room, but he said, "Thank you," and hoped she had heard it.

"When's the last time you ate?" his aunt asked.

"I don't know." He had to think about it as he continued to bend over Holly, watching her closely. Was that a twitch of her eyelid? "Food, right. I had a bologna sandwich last night, I think."

"I'm going to go see if I can get you a real breakfast. It might take a few minutes. Is that okay?"

"It's fine." He tore his eyes off his daughter and tried to give Sherryl a smile. "I mean, thank you. That's thoughtful."

"I'm hungry too. I'll find something here if I'm lucky. If not, I may pop out to a fast food joint."

"Sure. Anything is fine."

After Sherryl left, Greg pulled the uncomfortable chair closer to the bed so that he could touch Holly and watch her more carefully. Her legs moved and, once, her hand with the IV in it flopped over. He took it and turned it back over, making sure that the needle was still in there. Her eyes stayed open, and he kept expecting it to mean she was awake, but it didn't. They were just propped open. She blinked from time to time.

The doctor arrived, yawning, about forty minutes later. "Sorry I haven't shaved yet. I wanted to get right in," he said.

"I appreciate it." Greg got up and moved away from Holly to let the doctor examine her. But he couldn't stop himself from asking, only a minute later, "Is she waking up?"

"Give me another couple minutes here," the doctor said.

Greg bit his lip to keep the words he wanted to say from coming out. He wanted to beg, to demand that the doctor say something positive. Knowing that was irrational didn't stop him from feeling that way.

It took ten minutes for the doctor to run through his tests. When he was done, he turned to Greg. He wasn't smiling.

Greg's heart fell.

"I'm guardedly optimistic."

"Meaning?"

"Her Glasgow is up. I'm going to have her MRIed again this morning, to be sure, but at this point, I doubt she'll need surgery."

That was something. "Why are her eyes open?"

"Sometimes, they are."

"But how long could she stay like that, in a coma, with open eyes?"

"Years, I'm afraid."

Greg was expecting him to say something like "two days," and this answer was a blow. He groped his way back to the recliner and sat down. He realized he was breathing hard.

"But, as I say, we have reason for hope now. Any change—and these are positive changes—tells us that change is happening inside her brain."

Greg was still stuck on the concept of "years." Years of a coma meant something awful. "How long do we have? Until there's permanent damage."

"I'm sorry, Mr. Duncan, but there's just no way to know the extent of the cognitive damage until she wakes up."

"Guess."

"I really can't. But I can tell you children seem to recover at much higher rates than adults."

The reality of it was starting to force its way through his guilt and fear. He could imagine the future, Holly needing years of rehabilitation. Or losing the sunny personality of his daughter altogether, having her at home, dull-witted, unable to manage regular school. And him a single parent, trying to cope with it. After that, a lifetime of menial jobs for her. His thoughts were a rising flood of despair.

"I know it's hard to be patient. Impossible, really," said the doctor. "But there's no reason to quit hoping."

"If she wakes up, what will you be looking for? In her— cognitive function," he said, fumbling with the doctor's cold term.

"If she can talk, that would be great. Anything else—or almost anything—can be rehabbed. If she can see you, recognize you, and say words even at an earlier stage of language, that would mean good things."

"Give me a number. What are her chances? Of waking up and living a pretty normal life? Walking, talking?"

The doctor sighed, as if he had been through this many times before. And he probably had. "Fifty-fifty."

Greg wasn't sure to be horrified or relieved.

"And what are the chances she'll never recover? That she'll die or be a vegetable?"

The doctor hesitated. "This is pure statistics, you know."

"Okay. I know you aren't making promises. I get it."

"Twenty percent."

Greg moaned and closed his eyes.

"But that's based on her initial Glasgow. She's higher now. So there's really no reason to despair. I know it's hard to wait and see, but that's what we have to do."

"Do you have children?"

"I do. Two boys, 12 and 15."

It made Greg feel better, stupidly enough. He was probably a good doctor. He certainly had to be intelligent. He had come in before shaving or probably eating to check on Holly, so he wasn't heartless. "Thank you. I know you'll do everything you can."

"We all will. There are no better peds nurses in the city, I promise you."

Greg felt a tear run down his cheek, and only then knew he was crying. He wiped it off. "Sorry."

"There's nothing to be sorry about." With that, the doctor left.

There was everything to be sorry about. Most awful, that moment when the wind ripped Holly from his grip. He should have held on to her. He should have held her differently. Somehow, he could have prevented this.

He moved to Holly's side. Her hand had a red mark where the

doctor had been pinching her again, trying to test her reaction. He kissed it and said, "Sweetheart, I'm sorry. I'm so sorry I failed you."

She said nothing to that. What he'd give if she had—ten years off his own life, an arm, anything at all. Even if she looked at him and said, "That's right. You're a horrible father. I hate you!" How he'd love to hear even that.

Five minutes later, Sherryl came in with Styrofoam cartons with breakfast. Greg had no appetite, but he knew the day might get busy, so he choked it down anyway. "Thanks," he said, looking at the empty container and wondering what it was he'd just eaten.

He filled Sherryl in about what the doctor had said, and about his own fears.

She listened carefully, then nodded. "I know you want to worry, but see if you can't just keep your attention in the moment. Whatever happens tomorrow, or six months from now, you can't control. Just be here, and appreciate that she's still breathing and that there's a good chance she'll recover."

Unlike Jim, who wasn't still breathing. He felt bad for wallowing in his own worries. "Thanks. You're right."

"I'm going to take off now if you can spare me. Do you want me to get you anything after I see the funeral director and my minister? I could run by a Walmart and get you clothes that fit."

"That's awfully kind of you."

"It's really no trouble at all. I'm glad to have something to do to help you." She turned to leave and stopped herself. "Damn, I almost forgot. Your mother is flying back."

"From Australia?"

"Yes." She checked her phone. "She should be boarding about now."

"How long does it take? To get here?"

"Almost 24 hours."

Greg checked his watch. "Do I need to go get her when she

arrives?"

"She has her car in the long-term lot. Your job is to be here. And to take care of yourself."

"And work. I can't lose my insurance now."

"And work, though I don't know why you can't have compassionate leave."

"Maybe soon. It's still pretty crazy in town."

"I suppose I'll see that for myself." She smoothed out her jacket. "I'll be back in a few hours."

He went to her and pulled her in for a long hug. "Thanks. Really, I mean it. For everything."

* * *

The day dragged on, with Greg watching every little movement of Holly's. They took her away for an MRI, and Greg got out his phone and caught up on messages. He remembered to call Malika, and her little sister answered. "She's in the hospital."

"How is she?"

"Awake. Okay, Momma says. They'll let me see her tomorrow."

"No school today for you, eh?"

"No."

"Do you know which hospital?"

She named the one he was standing in.

"Thank you. Take care, now."

He checked with the nurse at the main station and asked how long Holly would be. When she said at least thirty more minutes, he asked her to locate Malika in the hospital and give him directions to her room.

He found himself in a crowded room. Both beds were filled. Two adult women and a teenage boy he'd met before were around Malika's bed. Malika politely re-introduced them. He stayed for five minutes, and when Malika asked about Holly, all he said was,

"She's hurt, but I'm sure everything will turn out fine."

"I'll pray for her," Malika said. "And for you."

"Thank you," he said, summoning a smile.

* * *

By noon, Holly's restlessness had increased to the extent that the nurses strapped the arm that had her IV to the side of the bed, so she wouldn't dislodge it.

Greg kept talking to her, hoping to bring her awake. He found himself telling her stories about when she was a baby. She had a growth spurt that left her banging her head on the underside of tables for a few months, and instead of crying, she had always given the table a dirty look, like it had hit her head intentionally. He reminded her of a picnic the three of them had taken when she was almost five, and they'd seen a possum carrying her black-eyed babies on her back, and she'd wanted to be carried on his back for the rest of the day too. He had obliged her until his back had started to ache. He reminded her of the fall play her class had put on, where she'd played a toothbrush.

His aunt came back about 1:00 with lunch, apologizing for being late. She handed him two bags of new clothes. "I know you don't have a uniform, but I found you a shirt that looks a little like it."

"That was thoughtful," he said.

"I cut all the tags off. They're at the bottom of the bag in case you want to return anything."

It startled him into remembering that she was paying for all this. He pulled out his wallet and handed her two twenties. "It's all I have on me right now."

She refused to take it. "Don't worry about it. It's a gift."

"I can't let you—"

"Greg, seriously. I'm financially fine."

"Are you? You don't need help with the funeral?"

"It's already paid for, that and the cremation. Jim did it when he was diagnosed, and wrote out instructions and all."

"When is it? I'll make sure I don't have to work."

"Not until next Wednesday. There are a lot of funerals, and there was no rush on Jim's."

"How are you holding up? About Jim and all?" He was thinking of her worry that she'd done something wrong by letting him die.

"I'm okay. It helped, what you said. And I knew this day was coming. In a week or two, I might be able to see it as something of a blessing—for Jim, I mean. Not for me, necessarily."

"Anything you need from me, you know you can ask."

"All I want from you right now is for you to take care of Holly."

"I couldn't do it without you." He was aware of the minutes ticking off. He'd have to leave soon for work. He didn't want to. As little as he could do at Holly's bedside, as impotent as that made him feel, he'd still rather be here than anywhere else.

An hour later he kissed his daughter and left. But he left the best part of his mind and heart there with her.

Chapter 16

His shift at work was nearer normal than yesterday's had been, though it was all solitary foot patrol rather than car patrol. The rescuers felt they had recovered all—or nearly all—of the bodies in town by sundown. No one was missing, but there was still a possibility that a single hermit-type had died and no one yet knew.

The final death count was 104, with three times that many people so injured they required hospitalization. The streets weren't clear yet, but another day of the heavy equipment working would take care of that.

From 7:00-8:00, there was more food distribution for the police and National Guard. He ran into the woman who had left him her card and shared a sandwich with her. When he explained about Holly, and said it'd keep him from following up on coffee for a while, she said she understood. And she seemed to mean it. There was nothing of the flirt or manipulator about her. If a woman could be said to be 180 degrees opposite to his ex, this woman might be that. As he watched her walk away, he spared a moment of regret that they hadn't met at a better time.

Then he realized there never had been a worse time in his life. If Holly survived, this might be it, the very lowest of the low he'd ever experience. Bizarrely, the thought made him feel better.

His ass was dragging by the time he got off shift at midnight. Again, he went to Sherryl's house, showered, and changed into jeans and a blue T-shirt, the clothes she had bought him. He drove back to the hospital, realizing he wasn't really fit to drive. He was short many hours of sleep. Every day he went without eight hours' sleep made him slower, loopier. Even without the grind of worrying about Holly every minute, he would have been in bad shape. As it was, he was aiming for basket case.

When he got to the hospital, he made Sherryl go home and get some good sleep in a real bed. Turning to his daughter, he said, "I'm sorry, sweetheart, but Daddy has to nap. I'll be right here if you wake up."

* * *

The nurse woke him at 5:00 a.m., doing her rounds. He watched her check Holly and asked, "Any change?"

"She seems to be resting comfortably. I don't know if you were told, but she was given a mild dose of sedative last night."

"Won't that stop her from coming out of the coma?"

"No. That's not quite how it works. She was moving so much, the doctor ordered it for her safety. When it's entirely out of her system, she'll probably begin thrashing again. Don't let it alarm you."

"Does that mean she is coming out of it?"

"It could."

Greg wanted to demand *when* she would, *how* would he know, how much more disability would be caused by every day in the coma, and a dozen other questions for which he knew the nurse didn't have the answers. It took all his self-control not to ask them anyway.

Soon after the nurse left, Holly did begin to stir. Her eyes had been closed when he came in last night, but now they were open, as if she was waking and sleeping on a regular schedule in addition to the coma. He sat by her bedside and held onto her arm while he talked to her, dredging up more memories from their life together.

She kicked at her covers once, and he rearranged them, wondering if she was too hot, or too cold. Could she feel hot and cold? If she couldn't tell him, how would he know if he should cover her or not? He knew, though he hadn't thought about it much, that other people had suffered just as he did right now, that tens of thousands every year must live through this as a result of auto accidents alone. Other parents had sat at a bedside, just like this, racked with worry, wanting to be able to do something to help, having the worst fantasies run through their heads. How had they managed it? How could he?

Greg felt stretched to the end of endurance. He would have anyway, had he been a person in a civilian job, with a boss that would say, Of course, compassionate leave, take the week off. He knew that the death and destruction he had seen was working on him too, and the lack of sleep. His mind wasn't dwelling on the severed leg he had seen, or the crumpled bodies, or the smell of ruin. But it was back there, a weight, waiting until this heavier weight could be lifted.

He was, he had to admit, a total mess.

He wished he could shower and shave again, change clothes one more time. It wouldn't make Holly any better, but he'd feel a little closer to human. He settled for going down the hall to the restroom and washing his face and neck. He would have brought his Dopp kit here, if he still had one. Maybe he could beg Sherryl to run to Walmart and put one together for him.

The doctor had come in while Greg was in the restroom, and was finishing up his exam of Holly. "The MRI looked so good yesterday, I don't think we'll need to do another unless there's a significant change."

Greg said, "So her—whatever score is better?"

"Glasgow. Just one number, but that's good. Better is good."

"Why?"

"Watch." He put his hands next to Holly's head and gave a sharp clap.

Her head turned away.

The doctor did it again, and her arms moved. The doctor stilled her arms, made sure the IV was still in place, and looked at Greg. "Sound reaction. That's good."

"So she's coming up?" Greg imagined her in a deep, dark ocean, stroking for the surface, starting to see the light at the surface, struggling to break free and reach it.

"Probably."

"What should I watch for?"

"Good question. It's hard to see the transition, sometimes, especially when her eyes are already open like this."

"I've been talking to her."

"I wouldn't count on her talking back."

"Why not?"

"If they lose one ability, it's generally speech."

"Do they get it back?"

"Usually, with speech therapy. A few struggle with slurred speech, but children do far better than adults in this. The brain is still adapting in speech acquisition, so they're set up to learn."

"I see."

"Don't give up hope," the doctor said.

"I won't," said Greg, and he shook the man's hand before he left. Of course he wouldn't give up hope. It was all he had. He'd hang on until—He stopped himself from following that thought to the worst possible outcome.

He'd hang on.

* * *

Three hours later, his mother came into the room, took one look at Holly, and opened her arms to Greg. "My poor boy," she said.

Greg stood and went to her, feeling like a child himself. She wasn't the warmest of mothers, but now, with her arms around him, she seemed so. She rocked him, patted his back, and kept saying, "Poor baby. Poor Greg."

It felt better than he wanted to admit. How he'd love to hand over the responsibility to her. Funny, that, how even after more than five years as a parent, he didn't feel like a parent sometimes.

Finally, they let each other go.

"Tell me what I can do for you. Anything."

"It was nice of you to come home and cut short your vacation."

"Of course I came back," she said, sitting in the recliner. "And Sherryl said you lost your house too?"

"Yeah, but that seems minor, you know." He gestured at Holly.

"You can both stay with me as long as you'd like."

"I think Sherryl will let us stay there, and that would be easier for my work, if you aren't offended."

"No. Whatever you need. Whatever's best for you and Holly."

She was seldom so accommodating. "I really appreciate it."

"Tell me what happened."

He sat back in the hard chair, turning it so he could look at either his mother or Holly, and he told her the story of the first tornado, and then the second.

He was surprised to find himself choking up when he got to the part where the roof tore off. "And then the wind. Mom, I couldn't hang on. I should have held on. I should have never let her go."

She came out of the chair and knelt before him, her knees popping. She took his hands. "You did what you could. That's all any of us can ask of ourselves."

"But—"

"Now, Greg," she said, her voice moving from sympathetic to stern. "They said on the news the winds were something like 264 miles per hour. You said yourself the wind pulled entire adult people along the floor. You can't do everything. You're not Superman!"

He made himself take deep breaths and get control of his emotions. "I know in my head you're right. But I can't stop feeling like a failure."

"You're not. You're a terrific father. I wish your own father had been that good to you. And you do it all alone."

"You did too, after Dad left."

"You were nearly a teenager. Different thing altogether. You took care of a baby and a toddler. You did it by yourself, and you did it well."

"I wish I were better."

"All good parents wish that. I wish I had been a better mother to you."

"You were a good mother."

"Not great. I know that." She got back up with another crack from her knees. "Never get old," she said, going back to ease herself into the reclining chair. "I know I was too demanding sometimes. I could have listened better. You're a natural parent. I was not. Or maybe I was just too immature. Maybe I'm too selfish. Maybe I was resentful of your father's freedom. I don't know why, but I was never in danger of earning Mother of the Year honors."

"You did fine. I turned out okay, didn't I?"

"A testament to you, I think, more than to me."

Greg wasn't at all used to this version of his mother, and it was throwing him for a loop. At least it distracted him from the gnawing worry about Holly. He went to her bedside, leaned down to kiss Holly's forehead, and said, "Your gran is here. Wake up and talk to her. I bet she'll get you a present if you wake up."

Holly twitched.

But she did not wake.

* * *

With his mother and aunt both helping out, Greg felt as if things were more under control. When Sherryl came back, his mother left to buy him more clothes and the Dopp kit. She said she'd shop for Holly too, and asked Greg for all her sizes. Sherryl mentioned her church's clothing drive, and that there was another at the Catholic church in town. With two organized women around him, and with two of them to share the afternoon shift, Greg felt a little of the weight lift off him.

Just before he was about to organize himself to go into work, Malika came in the room, wheeled by her boyfriend Adam. "I wanted to come make sure everything was okay."

The nurse came in. "This is a little crowded for an ICU room. Can we keep it to two people?"

Greg and his aunt stepped out for a moment so Malika could be wheeled up to Holly's side. He could hear her talking, but not what she said. In a few minutes, she was wheeled back out. "She'll be fine," Malika said. "I know she will."

It was nice to hear such simple and pure optimism from someone. "Thank you. And how about you? Are you healing?"

"I had to have one dialysis session. Bad blood chemistry because of the injury. I tell you, it makes me want to eat and exercise right. It is boring to be all tied up with tubes like that. All you can do is watch TV."

"Don't believe her about TV. She had me reading her printouts about her condition," Adam said.

"It's interesting," Malika said. "I wouldn't mind being a researcher on something like this. They know a lot, but there's a lot more to learn."

"That's my Meek," Adam said. "Mind always at work." He looked at the back of her head with affection.

"Is your mom here?" Greg asked her.

"You know her. She's more freaked out about it than I am. So I sent her home to take care of the house and sis. Honestly, I was tired of calming her down. I think it's supposed to be the other way around, right?"

"My mom is helping," Adam said.

Malika nodded. "But I won't be able to baby-sit for a while."

Greg smiled at her. "Thank you, but I think I have that covered. You just worry about getting better. Will you be here long? I'll make sure I drop by to visit."

"They said three weeks, then three weeks in a rehab facility, which I think is doctor-talk for nursing home. But they said in six months, I won't even know it happened." She rolled her eyes. "I'll always remember it happened. But by the time I'm in college, I'll be able to walk across campus on my own."

Greg watched her go, feeling oddly cheered by her energy.

"Seems like a special young woman," said Sherryl.

"She is. I was lucky to have her taking care of Holly this past year."

"You know your mother and I will do whatever it takes, right? And your insurance may cover home healthcare workers, physical therapy visits, and all that."

"I hadn't even thought of that." Greg's mood dimmed. "I am not looking forward to insurance hassles. That's the last thing I want to think of, trying to convince those blood-suckers to cover Holly's care."

"Shh, don't worry about that now," Sherryl said. "We'll help with that too. And if they deny anything, we'll just sic your mother on them. She could wear down Gibraltar by bossing it around."

"She could," Greg said. "I'm going to say goodbye to Holly, and then get to work. Thank you so much for staying."

She shook her head. "It's my privilege to."

Greg went to kiss Holly goodbye. Her hair was looking dank and greasy.

* * *

Work was calmer, and finally the street lights were back on. He had another hour and a half to go in his shift when he got the call.

Chapter 17

"Greg." It was his aunt Sherryl. "Holly's awake."

"I'll be there as soon as I can." He was alone, downtown, patrolling on foot, trying to discourage looting of the damaged stores that still stood, many with plywood instead of windows. He leaned his hand on a piece of plywood and tried to still his whirling thoughts.

Call in to Dispatch first.

He hated having to take the time, but there was no choice. He radioed in. "I need relief," he said. "I have to get to the hospital."

The dispatcher put him on hold. He was surprised when Rosemary came on the line. He repeated the brief words.

"Your daughter?"

"Yes. I really need to go, Chief." He was braced for her sigh, and for an argument.

"Go."

"Nobody else is out here."

"The stores can be unguarded for ten minutes. Just go do what you have to."

Greg was surprised. "Really?" he said, thinking he must be dreaming this.

"Look, I know I wasn't sympathetic before, and that was

probably my screw-up. I was stressing from the enormity of what was happening, and frustrated as hell that I was trapped where I couldn't do any good. But I'm not a total bitch. Go, be with your kid. I'll cover it."

"Thank you," he said. "I'll be back for my shift tomorrow."

She said, "Call in tomorrow, midday. We'll talk about it."

"Thank you," he said again. "Thank you."

"Go."

He went, sprinting for his car, which he'd left parked on the south side of town, halfway between Sherryl's place and downtown.

He sped out of town. Just south of town, a car pulled out ahead of him, and he had to slam on his brakes, and when the bumper of the car came even closer, had to steer onto the shoulder in a spray of gravel.

He stopped there, shoved the gear lever into park, took a deep breath, and willed himself to be calmer. Dying in an accident on the way there wouldn't help Holly. He pulled out and stayed to the speed limit from then on, all the way to the hospital.

But his hands were in a death grip on the steering wheel.

* * *

It was after visiting hours, and a security person stopped him. He showed his badge and explained, grateful once again for how the badge got things done quicker for him. Up the elevator, and then speedwalking down the hall, which seemed endless, though it was only a couple dozen feet long. Into PICU, past a nurse, to Holly's room.

His aunt was there—her shift, not his mother's. She backed away from the bed and he found himself stuck at the door, unable to cross the last few feet. He looked at his aunt.

"She hasn't said anything yet," she said.

He crossed to the bed, leaned over, and looked down at his

daughter, her pale face, her half-shaved head, the greasy hair. Her eyes were open and she was staring up. It didn't look any different to him, just the same distant stare. He brushed her hair off her face. "Holly? It's Daddy."

Her head turned, and he saw something different, then, a spark of something in her eyes. She was there, behind them.

Her mouth worked, but nothing came out. Her hand pushed at her covers, futilely. He freed it. She moved the arm, but he could see she was having trouble guiding it. He held out his hand. "Take my hand, sweetie. Hold Daddy's hand."

She flung the arm around and hit his wrist, then her hand fell back to the bed.

"That's my girl. Try again."

The arm came up again, and this time he caught it. She didn't seem to be able to open her fist, so he gently pried it open and held her hand. "I'm here. Do you feel my hand?"

"Unn," she said.

Torn between relief and horror, he made himself smile, and focus on the fact that she was awake. Awake was better than in a coma. Awake was better than dead.

His aunt said, "The nurse said the doctor will be back in. I think he was home already."

"That's good of him." Without looking back, he said, "Has she been any better than this? Any movement? Any words?"

"Not yet," Sherryl said. "But the nurse said it can be like a slow waking." She didn't say, Or this may be as much of your daughter as you'll ever get back.

If it was, he'd find a way to be grateful. He'd make her life as good as it could be. What else could a parent do?

"Here, sit," his aunt said, and he felt the hard chair hit the back of his knees.

"In a minute," he said. He wanted to be as close to Holly as he could be. He smiled at his girl. "I'm so happy you're awake."

She made another grunting noise. Then her face screwed up.

She was frustrated, he thought. She wanted to be able to talk.

Or he was telling himself tales to make himself feel better.

The wait for the doctor seemed interminable. But as much as he'd wanted the man to arrive and check Holly out, when the time came, Greg had a hard time relinquishing her hand.

The doctor ran through his tests again. About halfway through, he began to nod, seemingly unconscious of it.

Greg's hopes rose at the small sign. He pressed his lips together to keep himself from asking for reassurance. It'd come, or it wouldn't.

The doctor finally turned to him. "This is good." He checked his watch. "Another day in a coma, and I'd have been less optimistic."

"Will she get better?"

"Almost certainly she'll improve on her own these next twenty-four hours. But I'm getting PT in first thing in the morning, as well. We'll push her, and she'll improve faster. Get those neurons firing again. Or rerouting, if they need to."

"Is there permanent brain damage?"

"There's no way to say yet. Let her get all the way to alertness, and we'll see what we have."

Greg imagined the dark ocean again, the one she'd been swimming in. She was not quite at the surface. She was out of breath, straining for it. But the light was around her, sparkling off the waves just beyond her reach. If he could reach into it and pull her up, he would.

"Can she understand me, do you think?" he asked the doctor.

"Probably, yes."

"Good."

The doctor turned back to Holly one last time and said, slowly and with careful enunciation, "I'm Doctor Bill, Holly. I'm glad you're awake. I'll see you tomorrow."

Greg stood by Holly's bedside, vaguely aware of his aunt saying something to the doctor. He didn't want to take his eyes off Holly. He grabbed her hand and squeezed it.

She tugged at it, and he realized he had squeezed it too hard and loosened his grip. "I'm sorry, baby." He leaned in and kissed the hand. "Daddy's just so happy to see you."

Despite his exhaustion, he stayed up another two hours, even after it seemed Holly had fallen back to sleep, eyes closed. He asked Sherryl to get the nurse, and he asked her if that was what it was, or if she'd gone back into a coma.

"Normal sleep, definitely," said the nurse.

"Thank you." He smiled at her, and she smiled back.

"Sit down," said his aunt.

"Oh gosh, I'm sorry. I've been entirely ignoring you."

"Don't be silly. Of course you have." She laughed. "I'm so happy, Greg. For you and Holly." When he had sat in the recliner, she handed him a sandwich wrapped in plastic wrap. "It's a Reuben, from Izzy's. Courtesy of your mother."

"She remembered." He loved those sandwiches.

"Of course she did."

"I should call her about Holly."

"I did already. She said she wouldn't crowd the room tonight, but she'll be here first thing in the morning."

"I'm sure you're tired. Thank you for helping. You can go home and get some rest."

"I'll stay. You need to sleep."

Greg checked his watch. It was nearly 1:00. "I'm sure if she makes a sound, it'll wake me right up."

"Exactly. I'll stay and keep an eye on her, and then you can sleep better."

He smiled. "I think I'd wake up anyway."

He could see she was torn.

"Really. You need to sleep, and to catch up on your own life tomorrow." He remembered Jim. "When's the funeral?"

"Five days away, still."

"Are you doing okay with that? With everything?"

"I am. Better, at least. I'll always miss him. But I hope he's in a better place now." She kissed his cheek, gathered her things, and left, waving off his thanks as she did.

Greg devoured the sandwich, thinking, If there is a Heaven, I sure hope they serve a Reuben this good. He pushed the chair back to fully reclined, and fell into a light sleep.

* * *

The sound of a nurse doing her morning routine woke him. When she had left, he checked on Holly—eyes still closed—took his Dopp kit, and went down the hall to the restroom. He grabbed a cup of coffee, which the nurses kept brewed for parents in the waiting area, and went back to his vigil.

When Holly woke, it was almost a normal waking. Normally, she came to slowly, and grumpily for the first ten minutes. Only after she'd been up a half-hour was she her typical sunny self. Watching her stretch and yawn and rub her eyes with her free hand, he could almost pretend it was any normal morning.

"Good morning!" he said to her.

Her eyes drifted to him. "Aa," she said.

"That's right, honey. It's Daddy. And it's morning. How are you feeling?"

She frowned and yanked at the arm that was strapped to the bed. The IV, he realized, was out now. His heart lifted at the sight.

"I don't know why your arm is still tied up like that. I'll ask if we can get it free. Would you like that?"

Her frown smoothed out.

"Okay, I'll buzz for the nurse."

When the nurse came back, she shook her head at herself. "I'm sorry. I should have done this a few minutes ago." She loosened the straps around Holly's arm. "All better, right?" she said. "The doctor should be in soon," she said to Greg.

He moved back to the bed.

When Holly lifted both her arms, his heart swelled. "Hugs," he managed to say, what she said when she wanted to be held, and he leaned over and drew her up as far as the machine wires would let him, holding her in his arms for the first time since the wind had snatched her away.

I'm so sorry, I'm so sorry. I should have held on to you tighter.

"Da," came the voice in his ear.

"Yes, yes," he said. "It's me, honey."

"Hunry," she said, her voice rough with disuse, the word slurred.

But it was a word! He tried not to cry in relief as he pulled back and eased her down to the bed. "You're hungry? We'll see what's on the menu here, okay?"

"Ba—" She stopped and frowned, and then he could see her concentrate and try to make her mouth work like she wanted. "Antate." She frowned again. "Pantate." Her little face went red with frustration.

He wanted to laugh aloud in joy. "Pancakes," he said. "Cakes," he said again, speaking clearly.

"Cates," she said, and then her face turned even redder.

"Flapjacks," he suggested.

"Fatjats." Her face scrunched up in a look he knew well from a few years back, a pre-tantrum look. She started breathing hard.

"I understood you, honey. And I'll try and get you some—" He sought a synonym that might be pronounceable but couldn't think of one. "Pancakes, if they have them, okay?"

She began to cry.

He felt so helpless. "Sweetie, it's okay. Everything will be okay, I promise." He leaned in to gather her up in a hug, but she pushed him away, with weak arms. "Okay, okay. I'm right here." He watched her cry out her frustration. It only lasted five minutes, and then she seemed worn out by it.

He hit the call button then. When the nurse came in he

explained what had happened and asked if she could eat.

"We have to wait for the doctor. But he already said we can try water this morning." She poured a glass of water with a straw, and handed it to Greg. "Take it slow." She backed off and watched him bring the straw to Holly's mouth. She tried to hold on to the glass, but her hands bounced uselessly off it.

"I've got it," he said. "Just have a sip." He guided the straw to her lips. She drank, and then she started coughing immediately.

"Not to worry," said the nurse. "She'll get the hang of it again in no time."

He followed the nurse out of the room. "So she has to relearn everything? Even to swallow?"

"I doubt that'll take more than two or three tries. It's just timing the sucking and swallowing. She's coming along. Really, don't tear yourself up with worry until we see how the day goes."

Easier said than done.

The doctor came in, did his series of tests, and when he pinched her this time, she said, "Ow!" in an indignant tone.

"I know," said the doctor. "Last time today, I promise." He jotted down notes and then motioned Greg out of the room. "We'll have to talk out here from now on," he said. "She's clearly picking up what's happening around her."

"She wants food."

"And I want her to eat. But we need to put that off until tomorrow. Today, we'll work on getting her to take water. Then juice. By noon or supper, a liquid meal replacement."

"So she's going to improve today?"

"Yes, she will. I'll come by more times today and check her progress."

"What can I do? She seems so frustrated by it."

"Understandably. The PT will be in soon, and she'll explain the most useful ways you can interact with her, okay?"

"Okay."

"And I'd like you to talk to a counselor here. I know you're going through horrible times—have been, and you'll be continuing to have emotional upsets in the days to come. It's good to have someone to talk to. Tell them everything bad, and then you can turn to your daughter and help her more. You understand?"

"I do. I just don't…. I mean, I never talked to a psychologist before."

"It can be clergy, if you'd prefer."

"No, not really."

"Just someone with professional skills, and experience in this, okay?"

"Okay."

"I'll have the nurse give you a handout."

"I appreciate it. And everything you've done."

"You're a good father," he said. "You're going to be really good with her recovery, I can tell."

Greg nodded, not trusting himself to speak. He shook the doctor's hand again. He was still suffering guilt from letting this happen in the first place. Then the light bulb went off—oh, maybe talking to someone about that would make sense. Someone who wouldn't just say, "Don't feel that way."

His mother came in soon after, and chatted to Holly for a few minutes. "I brought you a bagel," she said to Greg. "Should I have gotten two?"

He shook his head. "Tomorrow, they say." He took his mother out of the room and explained what the nurse and doctor had said. As she was starting to ask a question, a tall woman with black hair in a loose ponytail came up to them, checked the room number, and said, "Parents of Holly Duncan?"

Greg introduced himself and his mother, and she said, "Good. Let's go in—both of you too—so you can see what you're going to be doing these next few days."

Holly was obviously scared, but Greg explained to her that the woman was going to help her be able to go back to school and play again faster.

"Taut?" said Holly.

It took him a second. "Help you talk better again?"

The PT said, "Speech therapy. That starts tomorrow, a very nice man named Alfonse. You'll like him—he's funny."

"Jotes?"

"Yes, he likes jokes a lot," said the PT. "Let's start getting you better, okay?"

For a half-hour, the PT manipulated Holly's limbs and showed Greg and his mother what to do. She left them with a handout that showed it all again, illustrations, with blanks that said "Every ____ hours," for each exercise. She had filled them in by hand.

"I guess we have our work cut out for us," said his mother, reading them over.

"Work." It reminded him. "I have to call in. Can you stay with Holly?"

His mother nodded, engrossed by the handouts.

Greg went back and called in to talk to Rosemary. "Can I have the day off?"

"Let me call you back after lunch. I'm working on the schedule now and trying to get you some time off. Do you need it?"

"I could use it, definitely. There's all this physical therapy to do, and I'd rather be doing it myself."

"Call you back after one," she said, and hung up.

Greg and his mother worked all morning at stimulating Holly's body and mind. His mother went out for a half-hour and came back with a stack of well-used picture books. "We can read to her—do you think she'd like that?"

"Ask her," Greg said.

"Holly, would you like your gran to read you a book?" She held up each book and let Holly look at the cover. Holly raised her hand to point to the third one. "This one? You bet."

He watched his mother read to his daughter and caught a fuzzy memory of her reading to him, many, many years ago.

Doctor Seuss. Shel Silverstein. It was soothing to sit and listen. It was good to take a break. He had a sense of the work that was going to be involved in getting Holly better. He'd do the work, of course. But it wouldn't be easy. And somehow, in there, he had to earn a living, and look for a new place to live, and fill out insurance forms for his house and car and belongings. There'd probably be government forms too. He'd need birth certificates for both of them, no doubt.

Luckily, his wallet had been with him. Imagine trying to do all that without so much as a driver's license.

After the doctor's midday visit, his mother sent him down to the cafeteria to eat, and he had the first sit-down meal he had had since the tornado. It wasn't gourmet food, but it was hot. He looked around the cafeteria, saw all the faces lined with worry, and realized he wasn't entirely alone. Or, rather, he was, and no one could ease his own burden, but a lot of other people had his pain and fear right now. Some of those worried faces belonged to parents, others to spouses, others to children of the patients.

Somehow, this made him feel a fraction better. Like he was a member of a community of suffering, of worry, of love.

Rosemary called just when he was leaving the cafeteria. He went outside to take the call and look at the world again. In the distance, storm clouds were building, and he felt a chill of fear at them. It'd be a long while before thunder and lightning and black clouds on the horizon made him feel anything else.

"I've put you on a weekend relief schedule, if you can manage that. So two days' work, twelve-hour shifts, and then the rest of your time can be spent with your daughter."

"I—Thank you, that's generous."

"I'd give you compassionate leave if I weren't so short-handed."

"I can manage this. I have my mother and aunt to help, so it's doable."

"Good. How's your daughter?"

"Awake. Talking a little. Doing physical therapy."

"That's good to hear! People have been asking, so I'll pass it along."

"Thank you."

"Get back to your kid. I'll be in this weekend, so I'll see you then."

* * *

At suppertime, Greg watched as a nurse fed Holly a few spoonfuls of PediaSure and talked him through what she was doing. She let him take over and watched over them to make sure he didn't do anything wrong. She nodded her approval, took the empty glass away, and left Holly and Greg alone.

"Your aunt Sherryl will be here in an hour or so," Greg said.

"Wan' smash potatoes," she said, her clearest sentence yet.

He smiled at it. "Tomorrow, the doctor says. I'll get you anything he says you can have."

"Huds," she said, reaching for him.

The machines were all unhooked now and he was able to take her entirely into his arms. He rocked her, soothing them both. When he went to put her back down, she said, "Don' wet go."

He hung on to her, remembering again the wind snatching her away. "Never. Baby girl, I won't let you go ever again."

The End

About the author and team

Lou Cadle is fascinated with disasters, having been in a few, including the 1989 San Francisco earthquake. A year of work in paleontology helped inspire the series *Dawn of Mammals*. Cadle has been writing professionally since 1991, is on Twitter and Facebook and blogs at www.loucadle.com, where you can also sign up for the mailing list to get information on sales and new releases.

Thank you to my team of proofreaders, cover designers, and especially to my friend Guy, retired Vermont state policeman, who answered questions about being a first responder with a family to worry about and who took the safety off the Glock.

Made in the USA
Las Vegas, NV
11 August 2024

93677181R00143